Agent N3 started toward the right when a silent tongue of fire lashed out from behind the door. Something sharp, like a power-driven needle, struck his left shoulder and sent him spinning against the wall, knocking over the tables and extinguishing the candles, plunging the room into darkness.

A second silenced shot flashed from the same general location, splintered the table edge, and deflected into the wall a foot or so above Carter's head. Carter fired where he'd seen the light. The bullet whined, glass tinkled, and something heavy hit the floor.

There was dead silence . . .

NICK CARTER IS IT!

"Nick Carter out-Bonds James Bond."

—Buffalo Evening News

"Nick Carter is America's #1 espionage agent."

—Variety

"Nick Carter is razor-sharp suspense."

—King Features

"Nick Carter is extraordinarily big."

—Bestsellers

"Nick Carter has attracted an army of addicted readers . . . the books are fast, have plenty of action and just the right degree of sex . . . Nick Carter is the American James Bond, suave, sophisticated, a killer with both the ladies and the enemy."

—The New York Times

FROM THE NICK CARTER KILLMASTER SERIES

BEIRUT INCIDENT
THE DEATH DEALER
DEATHLIGHT
THE DEATH STAR AFFAIR
THE DOMINICAN AFFAIR
THE DUBROVNIK MASSACRE
EARTH SHAKER
THE GOLDEN BULL
THE GREEK SUMMIT
HIDE AND GO DIE
THE HUMAN TIME BOMB
THE HUNTER
THE INCA DEATH SQUAD
THE ISRAELI CONNECTION
THE ISTANBUL DECISION
THE KALI DEATH CULT
THE LAST SAMURAI
THE MENDOZA MANUSCRIPT
NORWEGIAN TYPHOON
OPERATION VENDETTA
THE OUTBACK GHOSTS
THE PARISIAN AFFAIR
THE PEMEX CHART
PLEASURE ISLAND
THE REDOLMO AFFAIR
REICH FOUR
RETREAT FOR DEATH
THE SATAN TRAP
SIGN OF THE COBRA
THE SNAKE FLAG CONSPIRACY
SOLAR MENACE
THE STRONTIUM CODE
THE SUICIDE SEAT
TIME CLOCK OF DEATH
THE TREASON GAME
TRIPLE CROSS
TURKISH BLOODBATH
WAR FROM THE CLOUDS
THE YUKON TARGET

NICK CARTER

KILLMASTER

THE ISTANBUL DECISION

180

CHARTER BOOKS, NEW YORK

THE ISTANBUL DECISION

A Charter Book/published by arrangement with
The Condé Nast Publications, Inc.

PRINTING HISTORY
Charter Original/September 1983

ISBN: 0-441-37484-0

Charter Books are published by The Berkley Publishing Group,
200 Madison Avenue, New York, New York 10016.
PRINTED IN THE UNITED STATES OF AMERICA

Dedicated to the men of the
Secret Services of the
United States of America.

THE ISTANBUL DECISION

PROLOGUE

Dr. Harry Beachamp made his way down the empty corridor toward the end door where two Marine sentries stood, their rifles in hand.

"Morning, boys."

"Morning, sir," returned one of the sentries.

"How's the patient?"

"The same," said the young man, motioning for Beachamp to raise his arms. The doctor complied with a sigh.

"You'd think some of us might be exempt from this constant frisking."

"You know the orders, sir. No one gets through this door without a thorough search. No one." He ran his hands over the doctor's clothes, finishing at the cuffs of his trousers. Then, taking out a small portable metal detector, he repeated the process all the way up.

"It's just that it's all getting a little bit tedious. How's Bernice holding up?"

"Lieutenant Green seems to be all right, sir," the young man said, folding the detector and slipping it back into his pocket. "Although it hasn't been easy with a spitfire like this one." He reached over and opened the door.

The room was sparsely furnished; a hospital bed, a nightstand, a dresser for clothes—all in white. White blanket on the bed, white curtains, the only dab of color anywhere seemed to be the blue-black hair of the young woman who sat in a wheelchair facing the window, her back to the door.

Beside her sat a Marine nurse, also in white, her face drawn, drained of emotion. When Beachamp entered, she stood up and came forward. "May I speak with you a moment, Doctor?" she asked. "Alone?" This last word was added with a note of urgency.

"Of course, Lieutenant, but I'd like to see my patient first, if you don't mind."

"Oh, yes," said the nurse, backing off. "Excuse me, Doctor." She stepped in the direction of the far wall, working her hands anxiously in front of her.

Beachamp came around to the front of the wheelchair and placed himself on the window ledge so that he could look directly at the young woman. He felt his breath catch slightly in his throat. Her amazing beauty always took him by surprise. "How are you feeling today?" he asked gently.

Her dark eyes glared at him.

"Pain?"

She didn't answer.

"I would imagine," he went on.

Again, silence. She glared at him, her eyes as vicious and alien as the stare of a snake.

He opened his clipboard as though printed there somewhere was the secret of how to make her talk to him. The words TATIANA KOBELEV appeared at the top of the sheet. Nationality: RUSSIAN; Referred from: CLASSIFIED; Duration of stay: CLASSIFIED; Personal history: CLASSIFIED; Medical history: Good health except for the spinal injury.

He closed the cover and tapped it absently with his pencil, still staring at her. Scuttlebutt had it this was the girl who had taken a potshot at the President and killed a Secret Service agent, then had been wounded herself in the scuffle. The press had been thrown off the track. They were told she had been killed. Another girl had been buried in her place; a diary had been "discovered" that showed a mental history of instability. Then, once the public had been satisfied, Kobelev was rushed here to the military hospital at Camp Peary under the strictest security.

But all this was speculation, grist for the rumor mill. No self-respecting officer would be caught dead repeating such tripe. Still, he couldn't help but wonder if maybe the girl's hard attitude didn't stem from fear of being shot by a firing squad at any moment.

"I'm not here to judge," he said to her, softly touching her arm. "I'm a doctor. You're my patient. It doesn't matter to me what you've done."

She turned and stared sullenly out the window.

He leaned closer to her. He had taken several years of Russian in college, thinking someday to be able to read Tolstoy in the original, but he'd given it up when it drew too much time from his premedical studies. He could remember only a little of it now. *"I want to be your friend,"* he said haltingly in her native tongue.

Her eyes flashed back to his, hate radiating from behind dark pupils.

He bent still closer, close enough now to feel her breath. "Believe me, Tatiana, I don't care what you've done," he said in English. "I'm a Christian man. I believe we are all equal in the sight of God."

Her lips puckered and she spat.

Immediately the nurse, who had been standing on the other side of the room, dashed forward. "Oh, Dr. Beachamp! I'm so sorry!" she exclaimed, pulling a crumpled tissue from the pocket of her uniform and dabbing the saliva from his face. "She is a wicked girl. Absolutely wicked."

"It's all right," the doctor mumbled absently. "Please." He took the tissue and wiped his eyes and the sides of his nose. "It's my own fault. They told me what to expect. I just refused to believe them, that's all. I won't make that mistake again, I can assure you," he added, straightening himself.

The nurse drew him into the corner by the bathroom. "Is it possible," she whispered, "that this girl's faking not being able to walk?"

The doctor drew himself up. "Absolutely absurd! Of course not. You've seen her charts, Lieutenant. You know the extent of the nerve damage she sustained. How can you possibly entertain—"

"The other day she indicated she wanted to urinate. I went to get a clean bedpan when I was called down the hall by an orderly who had an emergency on another ward. Ensign Poulsen. I believe you know who I mean."

"The accidental grenade detonation. Blind, isn't he? I understand he's taking it rather hard."

"He was hysterical, sir. He'd gotten hold of a scalpel from somewhere and had one of the nurses by the throat. It took all of us the better part of an hour to calm him down. At any rate, I completely forgot about this one. When I remembered, I figured she'd either be in agony or wet the bed by the time I got back. But she wasn't, sir! She never said anything about it. The bcdpan was dry and the toilet had been recently flushed!"

"Lieutenant, I'm sure you're imagining—"

"No! I know that toilet had been flushed because I'd left cigarette ashes in it and they were gone when I came back."

"Smoking in these rooms is strictly against regulations!"

"I'm willing to take whatever punishment you think is proper. But I'm telling you that girl is lying. She can walk. I'd bet my pension on it."

Beachamp smiled. "Before you end up poverty-stricken in your old age, Lieutenant, I think I should tell you that medically speaking, there is no way that girl could walk. It's absolutely impossible."

"Absolutely, sir?"

The doctor hedged. "There might be a very remote chance that the nerve endings were not severed. We may have missed it in our tests. But the possibility is so small it's not even worth discussing. And as for your toilet, I'm sure one of the men outside came in and flushed it and didn't tell you. Did you ask?"

"No."

"There you are. I'm sure if we went outside right now and . . ."

The woman clutched at his arm. "This girl is playing possum! I can feel it!"

Beachamp scrutinized her closely. "Is this duty beginning to wear on you, Lieutenant? Perhaps you could use some relief for a day or two. I'll speak to Colonel Forbes about a temporary replacement."

"Maybe you're right," she said, self-consciously withdrawing her hand from the doctor's arm. "Maybe I *am* imagining things. But I'll tell you one thing," she went on, turning in the direction of the girl who sat with her back to them gazing out the window, "there's something about her as cold as ice, and it goes all the way through."

"Yes, well . . ." the doctor muttered uncertainly, his eyes following the nurse's to the angular, unyielding back of the girl who seemed oblivious to their presence. "I'm afraid none of us is too fond of her. I'll speak to the Colonel."

Tatiana heard the stupid American doctor leaving, but she did not turn around. He and his asinine attempt at Russian! As though his vile tongue could do justice to the expressiveness of that language!

But she had to contain her anger. She had to keep her silence, build a wall around herself. And wait until the time was right.

And when that time finally arrived, she'd have to depend on instinct. Instinct her father had taught her to depend upon and use. Attack, he said. Attack and keep on attacking until the enemy can no longer raise his head. And then keep on—keep on until you've utterly crushed him!

She thought about her enemy—his face a pulpy mass of blood—and it made her smile. It was the face of Nick Carter, the man who had put the bullet in her back, the man she hated more than anyone in the world. Revenge upon him would be sweet when it came. And it *would* come. In time. In time.

She twitched her toes inside the cloth hospital slippers. Her secret. She had to keep it from these stupid doctors at all costs. No one could know, no matter how they tried to take her unawares, no matter how many pins they stuck in her legs. Nothing could spoil the surprise she had in store for them, all of them. She would exercise at night. She would do isometrics in bed to work off the weakness that had crept into her body from the weeks of lying and sitting in this disgusting room. Then, when the time came, she would show them how well she walked. And ran.

The first to die would be that sniveling nurse. She'd find out whom she'd been dealing with all this time. What a pleasure it would be to watch the light of life fade from those dull eyes, to let death swell that sharp tongue of hers and silence it forever! But in time, not now. For now she must wait.

ONE

Nick Carter, the man uppermost in Tatiana Kobelev's thoughts, was oblivious to the hatred being directed toward him from the hospital at Camp Peary more than three hundred miles away. He lit another cigarette and dropped the match between the seats of the small rehearsal hall located on West 49th Street in New York City, then focused his attention again on what was happening onstage.

The director had stopped the show to make a minor adjustment, but now they were underway again, working on a scene from the second act of Tennessee Williams's *A Streetcar Named Desire*.

Most of the actors were bad, some even terrible—stiff, uncertain of themselves, or so overconfident that their performances lacked balance and subtlety. But the young woman in the role of Blanche radiated power. She *was* Blanche Dubois. When she spoke, Carter could hear the harbor sounds, and smell the sweat and stench of the New Orleans slum. She was the epicenter of the entire production, and the director seemed to know it, checking with her time and time again as to how she wanted a scene done or if such and such a change met with her approval. Finally they broke for lunch, giving Carter the opportunity he'd been waiting for. He slipped backstage and knocked on her dressing room door.

"Who is it?" she asked impatiently.

"It's me."

"Who the hell is 'me'?" she asked, flinging the door open. She looked into his face, and her mouth dropped open in surprise. "Nick!" she exclaimed happily, throwing her arms around him.

"Hello, Cynthia."

" 'Hello, Cynthia'? This is all you can say after two years? I pine for you half my young girlhood and all you can say is, 'Hello, Cynthia'?"

"May I come in?"

"Yes, of course."

The room was packed with crates of costumes, wigs, and other paraphernalia. He lifted a copy of the script from a chair and sat down. "Hawk sent me," he said simply. "We've a job for you."

"Business, is it?" she said, disappointed. "I should have known. You wouldn't come all the way up here just to pay a social call."

"That's not true, Cynthia. When they told me you'd been selected for this assignment, I couldn't wait to get here."

"Really, Nick? If you weren't such a Don Juan, I could almost believe that. David Hawk. I haven't heard that name in a long time. How is the old bastard?"

"He survives. He's tough. He has to be. But this time he needs your help."

"I've heard that song and dance before. It seems to me I remember you and me hotfooting it across the deserts of Iran one step ahead of the Ayatollah."

"We appreciated what you did."

"Swell. I get a letter of commendation from the President, and I can't even show it to anybody. That, and a broken heart. Now you want me to do it all over again?"

"I didn't break your heart, did I?" asked Carter with a smile.

She had been leaning against the dressing table. She came to where he was sitting and ran a hand through his hair. "You're an asshole, Nick. You know you did. You made me love you, then you ran off to Algeria or some damned place and that was the end of it. Tell me, this job Hawk has in mind—will you be working with me?"

Carter stood up and took her into his arms. "Yes."

"Closely?"

He kissed her neck. "Very."

She made a sound low in her throat that was half groan and half sigh, and pulled away from him. "It's no use. We open in Philadelphia in seven days for a month's run, then we return here. I can't just walk out on them now."

"I saw the rehearsal. You're the best thing in the show."

"It's a big chance for me, Nick. I'm no longer just an understudy. I've been learning."

"It's important, Cynthia."

Her eyes never left his face. "How important, Nick? Tell me the fate of the world hangs in the balance. Make it easy for me."

"Your Russian is still passable?"

"I was raised over there, remember? Until my father defected."

"Who's the most important individual in the Soviet hierarchy?"

"You mean officially, or who has the most power?"

"The most power."

"I'd have to say the head of the KGB. Everyone's afraid of him, even the Premier."

"What if I told you there was a man standing in line to seize that power, a man so totally evil, so obsessed with destroying both his country and ours, that he makes Hitler look like a Boy Scout?"

The hate in his voice made her suddenly cold, and she tried to laugh. "You're not serious, are you?"

"Deadly. I tried to kill him once, but I failed to make certain the job was done. I won't make the same mistake again."

"Who is this maniac? What's his name?"

"Nikolai Fedor Kobelev."

The girl's face turned white. "Oh, Nicky!" she exclaimed.

"You know of him?"

She sat down heavily in the chair behind her. "I know him all right. His name has been a curse in my family for years. He was a cipher clerk in State Security. An opportunity for a promotion came up, and it was between him and another clerk. The competition didn't last long. The other clerk was found at home, stabbed through the neck. That other clerk was my mother. I was a year old at the time."

"I didn't know."

She shook her head, the memory hard. "He pulled strings, managed to shunt the blame onto my mother's alcoholic brother. Uncle Piotr is still in Siberia doing life."

Carter's hands fell to his sides. "I'm sorry," he said. "I wasn't told. If I had known, I would have requested they assign somebody else."

"No, Nick! I want to do it. I have to. Don't you see? I owe it to my mother and my family. If you're going to run an operation on Kobelev, I must be there."

Carter shook his head. "There isn't room on this assignment for personal vendettas. The man has to be taken out cleanly, professionally, completely. There can't be any slip-ups."

"I can do it, Nick. I swear I'll do exactly what you say. But I have to be there when you put the knife in him."

Carter sighed. There wasn't much time. Finding another actress might take months. Besides, Cynthia's resemblance to Kobelev's daughter was almost uncanny.

"All right," he said at last, pulling a card from his pocket. "Show this to the receptionist at the base hospital at Camp Peary at fourteen hundred hours tomorrow. I'm afraid we're going to have to do a little surgery on your face."

"I don't care. Do whatever you must."

He took her chin in his hand and looked into her eyes. "Good girl," he said.

The next afternoon Carter placed a call to an unlisted number in Washington, D.C., and was told the "subject" had been accepted and the "experiment" would begin as planned. Thus he knew that Cynthia Barnes, née Katerina

Burjeski, had made her appointment at Camp Peary and that the CIA-selected doctors had found her suitable for surgery. That night he packed a bag and caught a plane for Phoenix.

His eventual destination was a small dude ranch on the outskirts of Tempe. Ostensibly it was a run-down tourist attraction that had seen better days, but in reality it was a rest haven for the agents of AXE, the super-secret information gathering and political action organization of which Carter was a charter member. AXE was doubly secret, secret even from the Central Intelligence Agency, its funding hidden in a maze of budget referrals and footnotes, and finally tucked safely into the President's own Special Expense Account so as to be utterly untraceable. Carter had worked his way through the ranks to the designation N3, Killmaster, a name that spoke more eloquently than any job description as to his purpose and capabilities.

The Litchfield Municipal Airport in Phoenix is rather small, in spite of the city's size, with concourses for deplaning passengers at one end and a large lobby with a double baggage carousel in the center. At the far end, doors lead to the parking lot. Carter arrived at 9:58 P.M. exactly and went directly to the baggage carousel.

He was relatively sure the usual broken-down station wagon with Mesa Verde Dude Ranch printed on the door in flaking gold letters would be waiting for him outside to take him the rest of the way to Tempe, and he was equally confident the driver would have been more than willing to tend to his bags as well, but Carter much preferred to look after his own luggage.

Over his shoulder he carried a small leather bag that contained his toiletries and other personal effects, as well as whatever book he was currently reading, usually a foreign language grammar or contemporary political history. But it was his other case, a finely tooled handmade Brazilian two-suiter, that he missed most whenever he flew, and for which he watched now with a steady gaze as the carousel began to turn and luggage began dropping to the rail. This bag held the small arsenal of personal weapons he had about him always: a 9mm German Luger complete with silencer, affectionately called Wilhelmina; and a small, pencil-thin stiletto, Hugo, that fit in the chamois sheath he always wore on his forearm. He possessed one other weapon, dubbed Pierre, a gas bomb that fit high on his left thigh, almost like a third testicle. But it was plastic and was able to pass through metal detectors without so much as a beep, a feat impossible for the other weapons. They had had to be packed away and had been out of his grasp now for almost six hours. The effect on him couldn't have been stronger if he'd been walking around all that time without clothes.

Like a determined little train of cars on a roller coaster, the bags, one by one, rode to the top of the carousel, then tumbled down, presenting themselves with a *clunk* to the several dozen travel-weary passengers at the bottom who closed in to snatch them up as they rode by. Carter waited, waiting for the familiar outline of his bag, when suddenly he felt the eyes of someone in the crowd staring at him. The alarm bell in the back of his head began to clang, the danger signal tingling in every nerve of his body.

He gave no sign that he knew. Calmly he collected his bag and made his way directly to the men's room.

In the reflection of the concession stand window he saw a man in light slacks and sports coat separate himself from the crowd and move in the same direction, a telltale bulge under the left arm of his jacket. The men's room was deserted except for an older gentleman standing at one of the urinals. He didn't bother to turn around as Carter entered, selected the last toilet stall in line, put a dime in the slot, and went in.

He took down his trousers, sat down, and pulled the suitcase up onto his lap. In a matter of seconds the old man would finish up and go, leaving Carter alone in the room. That, no doubt, was what the man outside was waiting for.

Carter unlocked the case as the old man finished, walked to the sink, and ran the water. Then he stepped to the towel dispenser. It rattled loudly as he cranked out several feet of paper towel.

From under a neatly pressed pair of Yves St. Laurent slacks on the bottom of the case Carter retrieved a wooden box.

The door swung open, the bustle of the terminal suddenly filling the room. The old man had left. Another second and the door swung open again, this time admitting a man whose step was a good deal surer and more distinct than the old man's shuffle.

Carter held his breath while these new footsteps hesitated briefly by the door, then continued on.

Time was running out. Carter found the correct key and opened the box. Wilhelmina gleamed and smelled faintly of gun oil. On the right, also resting in the Styrofoam, was a clip, and along the top of the box nestled a stubby cylindrical silencer. Carter took out the gun and silencer and fitted them together, making only as much noise as absolutely necessary to turn their perfectly matched, well-oiled threads.

The footsteps stopped at the next stall. Carter picked the ammunition clip from the box and held it in his hand. The jingling of coins in a pocket gave Carter his cue. At the same instant the dime slipped into the slot and clattered through the door lock's mechanism, Carter jammed the ammo clip in the butt of the gun, using the sound of the coin to mask the metallic *clack* as he drove the clip home. The man entered the stall, and Carter levered a live round into the chamber and took off the safety.

The man in the sports coat faced the toilet, whistling faintly as the steady stream of his urine thudded into the water below, his ill-polished Florsheims sticking out beneath his pale trousers scant inches from where Carter watched under the lower edge of the partition.

Then the shoes left the floor. One was raised to the paper dispenser bolted to the partition wall. The bolts creaked slightly under the unusual weight. The other disappeared as it was placed on the toilet seat. Carter twisted around, watching the upper edge of the partition.

The half moon of the man's head appeared above the flat horizon of the partition, and Carter fired, the bullet making two virtually simultaneous sounds in the tiled bathroom: the *chunk* sound of the explosive gases being dissipated in the silencer; and the thud of the impact on the man's skull, like a strong finger thumping a melon.

The entire line of stalls shook violently as the man's body pitched backward. An interval of silence lasted only a split second, then there was another thud as the body slammed into the small space above the toilet, the gun clattering to the floor. It came to a spinning halt at Carter's feet, a huge Graz-Buyra, standard Komitet issue.

Carter quickly stood and dressed himself. He put the Luger in his jacket pocket and the Russian gun in his suitcase. Then he climbed the partition and peered down into the next stall.

The man was dead, had been since the Luger's bullet pierced the frontal lobe of his brain, passed through his skull, and blew out a large section of the back of his head. The partition wall behind him was splattered with blood, gray matter, and bits of bone. There was nothing to be done about that now.

Letting himself down into the stall, Carter hurriedly went through the man's pockets. A New York driver's license identified him as Josef Mandaladov, thirty-eight, and gave his address as the same building that housed the Soviet mission to the United Nations.

Carter had just stuffed the billfold into his own pocket when the lavatory door swung open again and two youngsters came in, talking loudly over a percussive disco beat that emanated from the "boom box" they were carrying. One of them went to the urinals while the other stayed by the sinks. Carter held his breath, not daring to move.

When the one had finished at the urinal, he joined his companion by the sink where the two of them talked for several minutes. Laughing heartily, they finally left, the sound of their laughter and the insistent beat of the music dying only gradually on the tiled walls.

Carter lost no more time. He continued searching the body until he found what he was looking for: a Frontier Airlines ticket that showed Josef Mandaladov had boarded the same plane as Carter at National Airport in Washington. He had been booked through to L.A. but had deplaned here in Phoenix, no doubt when he saw Carter getting off. This meant he had no idea of Carter's ultimate destination, and that the existence and location of AXE's rest facility here were still secure.

Carter stuffed the plane ticket in his pocket. Then, after making sure from the angle of the body that the blood seepage on the floor would be minimal, he pulled himself up over the partition into his own stall, gathered up his suitcase, and walked out, leaving Mandaladov's stall closed, the word "occupied" showing in the tiny window on the lock.

It would be ten or twenty minutes before the body was found, and by that time he planned to be many miles away.

He crossed the terminal and went outside. As he'd expected, the battered Chevy wagon was waiting curbside. Manuel Sanchez leaned against the door. His expression split into a smile when he saw Carter.

"Evening, *señor,*" he said, taking the suitcase and throwing it in the back seat. "Did you have a good flight?"

"Smooth as a baby's ass," Carter said, getting in and slamming the door. "Shall we go?"

The next day a short article appeared in the *Sun* saying an unidentified body had been found in an air terminal lavatory. That was all. Carter watched the papers for the next few days, but there was no follow-up. He assumed the man's Russian origin had been discovered, and the FBI had taken over the case, blacking out the news media. He also assumed the FBI would be more interested in finding out what someone from that particular New York address was doing in Phoenix than they were in who killed him. Therefore, the security net around AXE and its rest facility in Phoenix would remain intact, a secret even from America's own internal investigating agency.

And although the FBI might never unravel how a KGB agent managed to wander into a bathroom at the Phoenix airport to die, his presence there was no mystery to Nick Carter. It was Kobelev, who had the whole of the Executive Action branch of the KGB at his beck and call, making good on his threat to kill him.

And yet, to Carter's thinking, it was a stupid ploy, an

angry stab in the dark motivated by pure vengeance with very little planning, hardly worthy of a man of Kobelev's ingenuity and resources. It indicated the man was desperate now that his daughter was being held in this country and knowing he couldn't get at her. And desperate was just the mood in which Carter wanted him. Desperate suited Carter just fine.

Thus began Nick Carter's stint of intensive training at the Phoenix rest facility. It ended almost a month later to the day when he received a phone call from David Hawk, the acerbic founder of the AXE organization and the only man Nick Carter ever called sir. True to Hawk's well-known dislike for long telephone conversations, the message was terse: "She's ready."

TWO

Within twenty-four hours of receiving Hawk's summons, Carter arrived at the base hospital at Camp Peary. He passed through two of the security checkpoints unaided, one at the gate in front of the hospital and another just outside the elevator on the fourth floor. At the door to ward "C" he was detained while a gruff Marine sergeant made a phone call. In a few minutes a slender, distinguished-looking man in a business suit came out and introduced himself as Dr. Rutherford. He signed the sergeant's book, then led Carter down a long corridor.

Rutherford explained that Camp Peary was where the Company brought its military trainees from foreign governments, also its political defectors and persons in need of stringent protection. It was designed so that persons inside would have no clue as to where they were being kept, neither which country nor even which continent. Security here, the doctor told him, was airtight.

Carter listened patiently although he'd heard it all before. He knew, for example, that Tatiana Kobelev was being held in this very building only two floors above them.

Halfway down the hall the doctor stopped in front of a blank white door. "You'll have to continue from here by yourself, Mr. Carter," he said dryly. "I'm not allowed inside."

"Very well, Doctor. It was nice to have met you," said

Carter, putting his hand on the knob and waiting for the doctor to leave.

But he didn't.

"I've told your superior, Mr. Hawk, that I deeply resent not being allowed to participate in the final stages of our little project," he said, an edge of anger in his voice. "These things need a delicate hand or weeks of work may be sacrificed. I told him my security clearance is the highest of anyone in the hospital. And the unusualness of this experiment and the way it was run—"

"If David Hawk said you weren't allowed inside, I'm sure he had his reasons," Carter said, cutting him off. "I've never known him to do anything without good reason. Now if you don't mind, Doctor, I'm expected."

Rutherford scrutinized Carter's rugged features for a second, then realizing his complaints were falling on deaf ears, he abruptly said, "I see," turned on his heel, and left.

Carter waited a few seconds and opened the door. Hawk was sitting in a small swivel chair in the middle of the doctor's examining room, smoking a cigar. Across from him on the examining table sat a young woman in a hospital gown, her entire head wrapped in gauze bandage except for two small slits for her eyes.

"Come in, Carter," Hawk said gruffly.

"Morning, sir," said Carter.

"Good morning, Nick," said the young woman.

"Good morning, Cynthia," said Carter, recognizing her voice.

"Rutherford give you a hard time?" Hawk asked, getting up to make sure Carter had locked the door. "That's the trouble with the whole CIA—too many people think they have the need to know. I wish we could have used our own facilities."

"If you don't mind my asking, sir, why aren't we? This organization leaks like a sieve."

"Exactly what I'm counting on, Carter. When the time is right, we want to make sure the right information is being passed on to the target. But this part of it," he said, turning to

Cynthia, "must be absolutely secret. We split the face into three different sections and had a different doctor working on each. No one of them knew what the finished product would look like. Here," he said, handing Carter a pair of blunt-nosed nurse's scissors. "Why don't you do the honors?"

"Me, sir?"

"Just be gentle with her."

Carter began cutting the swath of bandage that ran along her neck, then worked his way up the jawline to the temple and across her forehead. The bandage fell away easily, revealing reddened, taut skin that was remarkably scar-free. When the bandage had been completely removed, he stepped back to get a good look at her. "Amazing," he said.

"Uncanny, isn't it?" remarked Hawk, producing a life-size photo of Tatiana Kobelev and holding it up next to Cynthia's face.

"I couldn't tell them apart," marveled Carter.

"Let's hope her father can't either. At least not at first."

"May I see a mirror?" asked Cynthia.

Carter retrieved a small standing mirror from the supply cabinet and handed it to her. She turned her head slowly from side to side, studying it from different angles.

"It's a nice face," Carter offered.

"It's not my face."

"You're still very beautiful."

"You can have your old face back when this business is over," Hawk said. "Meanwhile, you two've got work to do. I want you to start training together, get to know one another again, think like a team. In the meantime, word will be dropped here that we intend to move Tatiana to the St. Denis Clinic outside Dijon. Supposedly, a French surgeon will be there to do one last operation on her back. It'll be perfect, isolated, quiet. Kobelev won't be able to resist. He'll have to figure that even if it is a trap, it'll be the only time Tatiana will be close enough to the Soviet Union to make a grab for her. What he won't know is that it won't be Tatiana he'll be grabbing."

"You mean . . . ?"

"That's right, toots," interjected Carter. "You're the bait."

Carter didn't see Cynthia again until the following afternoon when they started their training together in a little-used loft in the hospital complex. By this time most of the redness was gone, and her face had returned to its natural color. The resemblance that had been striking before was now even more remarkable.

"You look just like her," he said when she entered the room. "I had hoped for a reasonable physical similarity, but this is really something. The only way I could tell you apart is your voice."

"I've been working on that," she said, pulling off her robe, revealing her beautifully proportioned body clad in a black leotard. "These Americans might not look like ogres," she said, lowering her voice half an octave and stretching her vowels, British style, "but they have the most bourgeois tastes."

Carter laughed. "That's her to a T!"

"Hawk gave me some tapes to study. I think I've just about got her down pat."

"You could certainly fool me."

"Could I, Nick?" she asked, her expression suddenly serious. "What about her father? Can I fool him as well?"

"You don't have to fool him for long, just long enough for us to take care of him." He smiled. She forced a smile, but the troubled look never completely left her face.

A brief silence descended, but Carter picked up the thread again quickly. "Hawk wanted me to take you through some drills to get you out of harm's way when the bullets start to fly. He says you're a bit rusty."

"Okay," she said with a shrug. She was standing very close to him, and her fragrance filled his nostrils. For a moment he was reminded of the night they had spent together on the desert outside of Teheran. It was a pleasant memory. They had been camped at an oasis. The Ayatollah's troops had lost track of them temporarily, and they had taken the opportunity to make love on a blanket under the stars. When they'd finished, they lay back in one another's arms, and listened to the grunts of the camels and the gentle wind bending the palms. Pleasant. But something else was tangled up with it, another unconscious association not at all pleasant, and it left him with a confused feeling.

"How shall we begin?" she asked. "Do you want to attack me and see how my defenses are? Nick? You with me?"

"I'm here. Just lost in thought for a moment."

"Attack me and I'll see if I can fend you off."

He reached out as if to grab her by the shoulder, but she caught his arm, twisted it, stepped through, and in an instant he was sprawled flat on his back ten feet down the mat.

"Not bad," he said, jumping to his feet. "Now finish me off."

She came toward him, a bullish determination in her eyes, and suddenly he knew what it was that had confused him earlier. The look in her eye, her hair, her face, were exactly the same as Tatiana's the night she had supposedly killed her father in their *dacha* outside Moscow. The menace and loathing that had seemed to fill her entire being as she came running from the study, knife in hand, and plunged it into her father's chest came back to him in a flash, along with all the hatred and dread he'd felt for her at that moment. Without realizing what he was doing, he lowered his shoulder, grabbed Cynthia by the forearm, and catapulted her into the air. She spun once, awkwardly, like a stuffed doll, and landed on the edge of the mat with a sickening thud.

As soon as he realized what he had done, he ran to her. "You all right?" he asked.

She groaned and rolled on her side, gasping for air.

"Lie back," he told her. "You've had the wind knocked out of you."

For several minutes she lay with her eyes closed, trying to breathe. Then she looked up. "You take . . . all this . . . pretty seriously . . . don't you?"

"It's the way you look," he said, helping her to sit up. "You reminded me of Tatiana and all I went through in Russia."

"That must have been rough," Cynthia said, finally getting a deep breath and feeling her ribs to make sure nothing was broken. "Hawk told me about it in a general way, but I never did get the particulars."

He sat down beside her. "Your friend Kobelev has come a long way since the days he was a cipher clerk. He's still ruthless as ever, but his plots have taken on a new ingenuity—an ingenuity bordering on sheer genius for death and destruction. We'd been watching his progress as a case officer, then administrator in Department S for some time. Then when they transferred him to Executive Action, we got worried, but he was still something of an unknown quantity. All that changed with the *Akai Maru* incident. By that time we'd realized things had gotten out of hand."

"Akai Maru?"

"A Japanese oil tanker. We found oil drums aboard that Kobelev had irradiated with strontium 90, one of the most toxic substances in the world. Our estimates said that if that shipment of oil had ever been delivered, the incidents of cancer in California would have increased fifty percent."

"That's insanity! It goes beyond espionage. It's an act of war."

"That's why he has to be stopped. Shortly after that we learned Kobelev, or the Puppet Master as they call him, was in line to become chief administrator of the entire KGB. If that had happened, his power would have been limitless. He's already professed a desire to see our two countries at war. He has some half-baked idea of seizing power in the aftermath of a nuclear confrontation."

"Is he crazy?"

"He may very well be. You wouldn't know it to talk to him, but he must be. Crazy the way Hitler was crazy."

"You talked to him?"

"I did more than that. I 'defected.' Tried to become his chief lieutenant. Hawk developed a plan for assassinating the son of a bitch by convincing the Russian intelligence I was a disgruntled CIA caseworker who wanted to work for the KGB. The idea was to get me close enough to put a bullet in him, then get out of the country somehow. We figured

Kobelev knew me from the *Akai Maru* and that he might be interested in having me on his side if he thought I was sincere."

"How'd you manage to convince him?"

"By giving them files of sensitive material we knew they wanted. Real files. We turned over some valuable information, put some agents' lives on the line, but we felt it was necessary to get me close enough to kill him. You see, we had a time factor. Another few days and the Presidium was going to make his appointment official. After that, as chief administrator, he'd have been under such heavy security we never could have gotten to him."

"Then I take it the mission failed."

"You might say that." Carter's face darkened. It was clear he took it as a personal defeat. "I was about to pull the trigger when Tatiana, his daughter, suddenly rushed in and stabbed him. I found out later it was all an act. She only pretended to stab him. It looked real and it sure convinced me—so much so I even helped her get out of the country to avoid prosecution for patricide, which turned out to be exactly what they wanted."

"It was all an act," Cynthia said, marveling at the scam.

"Every bit of it. We think even the promotion from the Presidium was phony. He set us up to get his daughter into this country so she could kill the President. And she damn near succeeded."

"Where did this happen?"

"In New York. Outside the UN."

"You mean it was Tatiana Kobelev who tried to kill President Manning in New York? I thought it was what's-her-name, Millicent Stone, the one who died. They published her diary and everything."

Carter shook his head. "The FBI fabricated the story. They had to. Tatiana is a Russian national, don't forget. If it had gotten out who'd really pulled the trigger, it would have strained things between our countries forever. It may have even called for a military response."

"So Kobelev had it planned from the beginning. Lure you to Russia to provide legitimate entry for his daughter so she could kill the President. Amazing."

"The man is diabolical. He has to be stopped at any cost."

"Poor Nicky," she said, gently running her fingers through his hair. "You look as if you're taking all this on yourself."

"I had a chance to kill him in Moscow and I blew it. He'd contrived this fencing match between us, thinking he'd humiliate me in front of his wife and daughter. He didn't know I was an intercollegiate champion for four years in a row. I could have run him through, but I didn't. I thought I'd get another chance. But if I'd skewered him then as I should have—"

"If you'd killed him in front of his entire family you never would have gotten out of Russia alive, and our side would have lost one of the most valuable agents it has. Don't be so hard on yourself, Nick." She leaned over and kissed him. It was meant to be a reassuring peck, but her lips lingered a few extra seconds, savoring the sensation.

"Do that again and I might not be able to control myself."

She put her arms around him, her hand resting on the nape of his neck. "What do you think I've been waiting for?" she asked huskily. Gently she pulled him down with her onto the mat. He smiled and followed her without the slightest hesitation as she brought her leg up around his, and pressed against his body.

For all her strength, she was incredibly soft, and in a few moments they were both nude, and Carter was kissing her neck, and her lovely breasts, her nipples hard now as her chest rose and fell.

"Nicky . . . oh, God, Nicky," she moaned softly, her fingernails beginning to scratch his back.

And then he was inside her, and they moved in an easy, graceful rhythm, like two athletes or a pair of dancers, their passion mounting, but gently.

She cried out in the end, her legs wrapped tightly around his waist, at the same moment Carter thrust deeply one last time.

They finished their workout around eight o'clock. Cynthia

put on her robe while Carter stood staring out the large arched window at the end of the huge room.

"What are you thinking?" she asked, coming up behind him and looping her arm through his.

"I was thinking how nice it would be right now to go out and eat Chinese. I know a nice little place not far from here."

"I can't leave."

"I know, but every now and then I get a yearning to lead a normal, everyday sort of life."

She squeezed his arm, and together they stared down at the puddles glistening in the streetlight at the far end of the parking lot.

It was raining over the entire eastern seaboard from Stowe, Vermont, to Charleston, South Carolina, but out over the Atlantic the clouds dissipated, and in Paris at this particular moment, the weather was crisp and dry.

With six hours of time difference it was already two in the morning Paris time, and in spite of the fabled "nightlife Parisienne," the city's streets were practically deserted. Even the legendary Champs-Élysée's traffic was light—a taxi, a private car, and of course, every now and then, a truck.

One such truck, a squat white one, pulled out of a narrow alley onto the famous avenue. Ahead was the Arc de Triomphe and a dozen streets to the east the Palais de l'Élysée, where at this hour the president of France lay sleeping.

Two men sat in the truck: Jean, the driver, a wiry little Parisian whose looks greatly belied his august physical strength; and beside him, Guillaume, older and heavier, his sailor's watch cap pushed to the back of his head and a Gauloise eternally stuck to his lower lip.

They turned left on the Avenue General Gallieni and crossed the Seine on the Pont Alexandre III. Here the city began to change, subtly, but significantly all the same. The streets became cleaner, the shrubs better trimmed, the sidewalks in perfect repair.

Jean turned in at the rue Avignon and slowed. The street was quiet, not a soul stirred. Under a line of chestnut trees Mercedes, Peugeot, Citroën, and Cadillac limousines were wedged next to the curb bumper-to-bumper. Beyond these were the house fronts, cold gray stone with thick wooden doors behind screens of wrought-iron filigree. Bronze plaques identified each: Ambassade d'Espagne, Ambassade d'Italie, Ambassade d'États-Unis. At this last building Jean cranked the wheel, and the big truck lumbered down the long driveway toward the back.

The row of refuse cans stood against the north wall surrounding the compound. Jean stopped the truck with a bounce and a hiss of air brakes, ground the shift lever into reverse, and when the rear bumper of the truck was within a few feet of the cans, stopped it again.

The two men climbed out, pulling on thickly soiled gloves, and began dumping the cans. They were halfway down the line when the sound of someone clearing his throat forced Guillaume to turn around. Standing at the edge of the truck's rear was a uniformed figure, his flat-topped hat making his head seem disproportionately large in the darkness. At his hip was a revolver.

"How you boys doin'?" the figure asked.

"*Comme çi, comme ça,*" Jean said offhandedly. He picked up another can, slung it onto the back of the truck, banged it empty, and replaced it.

"Where's your partner, Estaban?"

"Sick," said Jean. "*Mal à l'estomac.*" He made a face and a hand motion around his middle to indicate how poorly Estaban was feeling.

"Who's this guy, then?"

"*Permettez-moi . . . mon ami, Guillaume,*" Jean said.

Guillaume bowed his head uncertainly, watching Jean for his cue out of the corner of his eye.

"Yeah," said the guard. "Ain't you boys workin' a bit early this mornin'?"

Jean made several gestures to indicate he'd like to explain but couldn't because of the language barrier, then finally pointed to Guillaume and said, "Moonlight."

"I see," said the guard. "He has another job during the day?"

Jean smiled expansively and nodded. Guillaume, meanwhile, had moved behind the guard, had pulled out a piece of knotted piano wire, and was winding it around his hand.

"*Sa femme,*" explained Jean, making a big stomach with his hands.

"I get it," the guard said. "His wife is pregnant and he has to work two jobs. You poor son of a bitch." The guard put his hand sympathetically on Guillaume's shoulder as he turned and headed back to the house. "Well, try to keep the noise down, boys. Got people sleepin' upstairs."

Jean shot a glance at Guillaume. He shook his head.

In a few minutes they'd finished the last of the barrels, closed the truck, and were heading back up the driveway to the street. As he turned the corner and recovered the wheel, Jean slapped his companion brusquely on the shoulder. "Give it to me," he said harshly, holding out his up-turned palm.

Reluctantly Guillaume produced the piano wire he had in his pocket and gave it to Jean.

"You idiot," Jean said as he tossed it out the window.

Guillaume sighed to let Jean know he was restraining himself with only the greatest of difficulty, turned away, and spent the rest of the short trip staring sullenly out the window.

Jean turned left toward the Seine and crossed the Pont Alexandre III. Soon Paris became Paris once again. Narrow winding streets littered with bottles and scraps of paper, utility poles plastered with handbills. As they passed, the lights of the Café du Rive Gauche winked out. A drunken shout came to them over the engine noise, and a fight spilled out into the street. Jean steered deftly around it, then took a left into an alley and stopped at the far end of it at a green doorway lit by a single, unshaded bulb.

The two of them got out, put on their soiled gloves a second time, and began shoveling the used containers, bits of paper, and garbage from the back of the truck into three large wooden boxes that stood by the door.

As they worked, the green door opened and an angular

man stepped out, as thin as one could imagine a human being to be and still stand erect. On his gaunt face was a pair of large, perfectly round eyeglasses which gave him a peculiarly bug-eyed look. A thick cigarette hung in his mouth, and a narrow column of smoke wound its way along the ridges of his face as he watched the two men work.

"Trouble?" he asked.

Jean stopped shoveling. "He is the trouble," he said with a nod toward Guillaume.

Guillaume shrugged, and the thin man smiled wanly.

When they had finished filling the first of the boxes, they carried it inside and placed it on the floor next to a white screen roughly six feet square that had been laid out in the center of the room. Guillaume, who had been to this place many times but had never before been allowed to come inside, took the opportunity to look around.

The walls of the room were painted stark white with a black, acidproof countertop running around its perimeter. On the counter were various modules of electronic equipment, some with screens, some with only buttons and dials. Stacked on the floor below these were boxes, presumably with more electronic equipment. In one corner stood an enlarger for making photographic prints.

"Seen enough?" the thin man asked pointedly, coming up behind him.

Guillaume swept his eyes over the smaller man's emaciated frame. It wouldn't take much to crush him like a piece of scrap paper.

"Your job is to bring in the garbage. You're a garbage collector. Don't forget it."

Guillaume grunted and left. When he and Jean returned with the next box, the thin man had overturned the first load onto the white screen and was picking through it on his hands and knees.

After they'd gone, the thin man walked to the phone and dialed. As it was ringing, he snuffed his cigarette in the ashtray.

"Hello?" said a voice.

"Charles."

"Hello, Charles. Find something?"

"Yes. Tell the man I think I may have found what he's looking for."

"Excellent, Charles. And the men driving the truck?"

"Jean and Guillaume."

"They will be taken care of."

Charles hung up the phone and scrutinized the image on the screen of the projection microscope again. He smiled.

THREE

The telephone sounded far away and indistinct, as though someone had stuffed it with cotton. Carter rolled over and picked up the receiver from the nightstand.

"Code ten," said Hawk's voice.

Carter came immediately awake. "Yes, sir," he said. He pressed the hold button and went to the closet where he began working the combination to the safe.

From the safe he pulled out what looked to be an ordinary leather briefcase and carried it back to the bed. Along the way he picked up one of his shoes from underneath the valet.

He laid the briefcase on the bed, then taking the shoe in hand, twisted the heel. It separated neatly into halves, the bottom one having embedded in it a thin plastic circuit card. He slipped out the card and inserted it into a slot in the briefcase. Its locks snapped open.

Inside the lid was a small library of cassette tapes. Carter selected the one labeled "10" and fitted it into the console that made up the lower half of the case. This consisted of a smooth deck of burnished aluminum broken only by a power switch, condenser microphone, volume control, and the usual buttons found on any cassette tape recorder—these, and one other item slightly more unusual. At the top of the set was an indented cradle such as those found on a telecopier, with two back rubber suction cups marked RECEIVER.

Carter untangled the tiny microcircuit headphones,

plugged them in, put the phone receiver into the cradle, hit the play button, and took the phone off hold. Hawk said, "Can you hear me?"

"Yes, sir."

"Kobelev has lost his *dacha* outside of Moscow."

"Lost it, sir?"

"Had it confiscated."

"Has he been arrested?"

"Negative."

"What's the analysis?"

"Apparently, the Presidium is taking a conservative turn. The failure to kill President Manning and the risk of all-out war must have sobered them."

"Any possibility of help from that quarter?"

"I doubt it. Kobelev may not command the clout he once did, but he's still at large and extremely dangerous. That may be why the Presidium stopped short of cutting him down completely. Perhaps they're afraid of him."

"What's all this mean to us?"

"It means if Kobelev wants his daughter, he'll have to come for her himself. He doesn't have the resources any longer to delegate that kind of responsibility. Which works in our favor and which brings me to the second development."

"Which is?"

"He wants to talk."

"A defection, sir?"

"Strange you should ask. That's one of the possibilities I've been considering."

"It might also be a trap."

"That's the other possibility, especially since he asked for you, specifically. But the official message says he wants to work out a trade for Tatiana. Remember Nikolai Sachs?"

"The scientist?"

"One of the leaders of the principal dissident movement among the Moscow elite. Mikhail Zoshchenko?"

"Jewish writer. Jailed for blowing the whistle on Stalinist anti-Semitism."

"Right. And you know Maria Morgan, the CIA double

they tumbled to in '68. We'd like nothing better than to get the chance to debrief her."

"Big names," said Carter. "They'd certainly look good coming over, but can Kobelev still pull it off, especially since he's fallen from grace?"

Hawk sighed. "Frankly, I don't know. I do know that Zoshchenko and Maria Morgan have been moved from Tomak to Tashkent, presumably to make them more accessible should a deal be worked out."

"You're not seriously suggesting we talk with this man?"

"Let's get one thing straight, N3. Nothing's changed. If you go into this, you go as an assassin, not a negotiator. The man's to be killed at any cost—*any cost*. Those orders come from upstairs."

"Yes, sir."

"But if there's a chance we can catch him out in the open without having to expose ourselves any further, we're going to have to take it."

"Where's the meet?"

"Berlin. A safe house has been arranged just on the east side of the wall."

"That is his territory, sir."

"That's right. It's his ball game in his park. Maybe he feels safer that way. When you hit him, you're going to have to get out of there somehow. I know you've managed that before."

"If he's there, I'll take him out."

"All right, Carter. Not too confident. We want you coming back from this. In the meantime we're going ahead with the switch in Dijon. I've already arranged to feed Kobelev the fact that Tatiana will be in France. You remember Ned Cassidy?"

"CIA caseworker in Central America. Instrumental in keeping Castro's influence to a minimum down there."

"He's going over tomorrow."

"Defecting, sir?"

"No. He's going freelance. Selling whatever to the highest bidder. He has the complete file on Tatiana, present physical condition, prognosis, whereabouts, what we plan to do with her, the works. We'll give Kobelev three days to process the information. Then, depending on how things go in Berlin, we'll be ready for him."

"I guess so, sir."

"Doubt in your mind, Carter?"

"Well, sir, it's just that there'll be a couple of days when I won't be around in case something happens to Cynthia."

"I understand your concern. But it's important to give our target the information on Dijon as soon as possible. If he *is* thinking of showing up in Berlin, he'll know we've moved her closer to his border, and he'll think we're coming in good faith."

"Yes, sir."

"You're on the early flight out of National. Your tickets are at the desk. Your contact in Berlin is Ronald Kliest, our station head in the area and an expert at getting people back and forth over that wall. He may prove useful."

Hawk rang off without waiting for a reply, and for a moment Carter sat on the edge of the bed, thinking. Then he quickly put the decoding device away and dressed in wool trousers and a wool sports coat. A bag, always packed, lay under the bed. He brought it out, checked its contents, and added his weapons. When he was ready, he called a cab.

At the Air France desk at National he traded his ticket for a one-way to New York. At Kennedy he would buy another ticket for a direct flight into Tegel Airport, which is the secondary field across Berlin from the main terminal at Tempelhof. In this way no one, not even Kliest, would know when or where he was coming into town.

In New York he watched each passenger as the plane loaded for some sign he or she wasn't all he or she pretended to be, but everything seemed innocent and aboveboard. No one made the connection between the Washington flight and the flight to Berlin. And yet still he was wary. He had no wish to go through a repeat of what had happened in Phoenix.

It was late and a light rain was falling when he arrived at Tegel. The customs officials didn't bother opening his bag, choosing instead those of a wealthy, nervous-looking German woman who was standing next to him. If they had bothered, they would have no doubt found the Luger, but it would have been of no great consequence. Carter carried identification as a gun collector, and while a Smith & Wesson or Colt might have stirred suspicion, in Germany there was no reason to explain possession of a Luger.

He collected his bag and carried it out to the line of waiting taxis. He selected the third in line, got in, and gave the driver Kliest's address.

Kliest had no doubt met the flight at Tempelhof that had arrived earlier, not found Carter, and returned home. Consequently, he should be there waiting when Carter pulled up.

After having surveyed the house from the cab, Carter got out a block further down, paid the driver, and went into a small *biergarten* across the street. He ordered a stein, paid for it, and sat down by the rain-streaked window to watch the house a while longer.

For more than an hour no one came or went, the only sign of life being a light in the living room window. At ten o'clock this winked out. Carter snuffed out his cigarette, finished the last of his second beer, hoisted his bag, and crossed the street.

A light rap brought Kliest to the door immediately. "*Wer ist da?*" he asked suspiciously.

"Carter."

"Ach!" he exclaimed, throwing the bolt back and opening the door. "I've been expecting you. I thought there'd been a change of plan."

"I'm sorry I wasn't at the airport. I had to make sure I wasn't followed," Carter said, stepping inside.

"Of course. Of course. Let me take that," said Kliest, grabbing the suitcase and standing it by the wall.

It was a modest home. A hall off the living room apparently led to the bedrooms. To the left behind a counter was the kitchen. A wooden train set on the floor indicated small children, and Carter remembered an entry in Kliest's dossier, something about a son he doted on.

"How was the flight?"

"Quiet."

"Sit down. Sit down." Kliest indicated a leather armchair, and Carter eased himself into it. "I'm sorry my wife isn't up. She very much wanted to meet you."

"Maybe it's just as well. I've a lot of work ahead of me tonight. Hawk tells me you're pretty good at getting people back and forth across the border."

Kliest shrugged in a self-deprecating way. His glasses and balding head made him look like a slightly-less-than-successful businessman, and the gesture suited him. "We've had our triumphs. Our setbacks, too."

"Can you get me across tonight?"

"Tonight? Ach, no—impossible. The ports of entry are all closed by eight."

Carter took out a cigarette, then picked up a lighter from the end table and lit it. "That's very disappointing. I was told you could arrange such things."

"*Mein Herr,* there is no difficulty getting you into the Eastern Sector. The problem lies in getting you out. As a foreigner, you may enter at either of the two checkpoints with no more than your passport. But your name will be kept on record, and if you do not check in within a specified time, a warrant is issued for your arrest. But this needn't concern us. Everything has been arranged. Here." He reached behind his chair, pulled out a long metal object and handed it to Carter. "What does that look like to you?"

"A tripod, most likely for a camera, judging from the screw connection at the top."

"Wrong, my friend. Let me show you." He twisted one of the legs off the stand and pulled it into two pieces along a seam that had been so cleverly made as to be almost invisible. He laid these parts on the floor and began undoing another leg. In less than a minute he had the entire device in pieces on the floor and was reassembling it.

"I have a workshop downstairs," he explained. "I made this up when I heard you were coming. Fabricating 'tools of the trade' is something of a hobby of mine."

As the reconstructed object began to take shape, Carter smiled. "It's a rifle," he said.

Kliest fitted the last of the tripod parts along the stock and handed it to Carter. Carter swung it up quickly and aimed down the tripod leg barrel at the wall. "It even has a certain balance," he said softly.

"There's more," said Kliest. He fetched a camera from a desk drawer across the room, took the rifle from Carter, and fitted the camera's telephoto lens along a slot that had been discreetly machined in the barrel's top. "Now try it."

"It's perfect," marveled Carter, sighting a table lamp a few feet away.

"I have had papers made up identifying you as Wilhelm Schmidt, professional photographer. You can enter the Eastern Sector tomorrow, make your appointment and leave. No one will be the wiser."

Carter shook his head. "You forget I'm as much the hunted in this as I am the hunter. And the time and the place have been arranged. I have to get over there tonight to take advantage of what little element of surprise I have left."

"And how will you get out? You'll have to go over the wall."

"You said you've had some success with that."

"Some," said Kliest, taking the rifle from Carter and, with an air of disappointment, beginning to dismantle it. "But we had time to prepare, to wait for the right conditions. Sometimes months. I doubt it can be done on such short notice."

"We'll just have to try. Tell me more about these checkpoints. How many guards are there and how well armed?"

For the next hour Carter pumped his host for every scrap of information he could ferret out on conditions along the wall—guards' timetables, gun emplacements, minefields, buildings nearby, their contents and accessibility, and at the end of the hour, Carter sat back thoroughly frustrated. "There must be some way over short of creating an international incident," he declared.

"*Mein Herr*, some of the best minds in Germany have been trying to crack that nut for more than thirty years. Believe me, the wall is virtually impregnable."

"I don't believe it," said Carter. "I refuse to believe it."

He picked up a section of the tripod gun and rolled it absently in his hand. "Nice piece of work, this," he said. "Why don't you take me downstairs and show me your workshop? Maybe if we get our minds off the problem for a while, a solution will present itself."

They entered the basement down a stairway from the kitchen. Kliest turned on a series of overhead fluorescents, and Carter was amazed at the number of power tools the man had at his command. "You must have a small fortune invested down here," he said.

"You've been talking to my wife," said Kliest. "She's always complaining about the money I spend on my crackpot inventions."

"What's in there?" Carter asked, indicating with a nod the door on the other side of the room.

"Materials."

Carter opened the door and switched on the light. Stacked on shelves and piled in wooden bins were sections of pipe, pieces of various metals, jars of paint, odd chunks of wood.

"Mostly what's left after I've put something together," said Kliest, peering in over his shoulder.

"What's this?" Carter asked, pulling something from a lower shelf.

"A nylon tent someone was throwing away. I haven't found a use for it yet."

Carter ran his hand over the material. "Lightweight, strong. It gives me an idea, Herr Kliest. Most definitely, an idea."

Carter led the way into the workshop to a drafting table that stood in a corner. Taking out a pad he made a quick sketch, then pushed it over to Kliest.

"It could be done," said Kliest, stroking his chin. "It's never been tried, and for that reason it may work. It'll take some time."

"Tonight?"

"Yes, tonight."

Carter stripped off his jacket and the two men set to work. It was after one o'clock by the time they finished.

"We should test it, of course," Kliest said, wiping his hands with a rag.

"We haven't the luxury," said Carter. "I'll fold it up and put it in its case. You get the car."

While they'd been working, Kliest had told Carter of a freight train that ran nightly into the Eastern Sector. It was not inspected because it was assumed no one would want to sneak *into* East Berlin. On the return trip, however, it was carefully gone over by guards and dogs, and over the years many people had been arrested trying to escape. The train slowed to a comfortable fifteen kilometers per hour under the Spandau Bridge as it steamed around the rail yards at Reinickendorf. The Spandau Bridge was only ten minutes from Kliest's house by car.

When Kliest returned downstairs, Carter was just finishing. On the floor at his feet lay a cylindrical object seven feet in length and ten inches in diameter covered with a lightweight nylon casing. Attached to either end was a shoulder strap to facilitate carrying.

The two of them stared down at the cylinder. "I'll bet anything it works," Carter said.

"You are betting, *mein Herr*. You are betting your life."

The Spandau Bridge is one of the few in the city to have survived World War II. Decades of engine smoke have blackened it, and tons of coke dust have settled on it from the iron foundries across the canal. In the drizzling rain it gave off a sulphurous smell.

Carter looked down at the eighteen sets of tracks gleaming in the yard lights. "How do I know which track the train will come on?" he asked.

"Numbers eight and ten are through traffic," said Kliest. "All the others are for switching in the yard."

"Thanks," Carter said, then added, "for everything."

"Good luck, *mein Herr*."

"If you don't hear from me in twenty-four hours, burn my suitcase and everything in it."

Kliest nodded solemnly. They were standing on the bridge

embankment just off the road. Kliest turned and trudged back up toward the car. In the distance a train whistle sounded, accompanied by the faint chattering of wheels against the rail.

Kliest stopped before reaching the top of the embankment and turned around. "Do you remember the address in the Eastern Sector?" he asked.

"Fourteen Mariendorfstrasse."

"And the Brandenburg?"

"At the end of Unter den Linden. That won't be hard to find."

Kliest nodded approval. The train was getting closer. "Good luck," he repeated.

Carter, with the long cylinder dangling from his back, began the arduous, hand-over-hand climb up the girders that formed the underside of the bridge.

The engine's headlight wobbled in the distance. It had rounded the curve at the far end of the yards and was beginning the straightaway that would bring it under the bridge.

Carter, watching its progress and realizing he might be late, began to scramble from girder to girder. The metal was wet from the rain and slippery underfoot. Twice the cylinder caught in the metal framework, and he had to stop and wrench it free.

The big engine passed underneath just as he got himself in place, rattling the bridge and nearly suffocating him with diesel exhaust. A string of boxcars followed with flat, hard roofs slick with rain. He watched them rattle by ten or so feet below and wondered if even fifteen kilometers an hour wasn't too fast. Next came flatcars loaded with farm equipment: tractors with sharp, gleaming plow blades. To fall onto these would mean certain death.

He looked down the train. Making the corner were a series of gondola cars loaded with coal. He disentangled the cylinder strap and let himself down until he was hanging from the girder by his hands. He let the first one pass, getting his timing on the second, then he let go. He hit the coal mound just below its peak, tumbled down it, and stopped with his back up against the well of the car. He pulled himself upright and took account of things. No bones broken, and the package seemed to be intact. He pulled it close to him, turned his collar up against the wind, and sat back to wait.

Twenty minutes later he felt the cars grinding to a halt. They had come to an outpost on the track. A barbed-wire barrier ten feet high extended up the embankment on either side, and on the track were a guardhouse and a gate. The gate was open and the train finally stopped just in front of it, no doubt for the guard and the engineer to exchange bills of inventory.

Ten minutes passed and the train started up again. Carter waited until he was well past the guardhouse, then jettisoned the cylinder and jumped, landing in the tall grass. He ran back and retrieved the cylinder, then scrambled up the embankment to the road.

He had made it. He was in the Eastern Sector. All that remained now was to find the building in which the meeting with Kobelev was scheduled to take place and scout it out. If Kobelev showed up at the appointed time, he'd kill him. If not and it was a trap, at least he'd know about it in advance.

FOUR

Sister Marie-Thérèse kneeled before the crucifix in the chapel of the St. Denis Clinic and mumbled a Hail Mary. It had been a while since she'd prayed, and when she found herself rushing through it, she stopped and chided herself for a lack of piety. It was this new patient on the third floor. The young woman kept her running all day. After the seventh or eighth trip up those stairs, her joints got stiff.

Supporting herself with a gnarled hand on the altar top, she pulled herself slowly erect, turned, and eased herself into one of the wooden pews behind her. Then with a sigh she sat back and stared at the crucifix, not seeing it really, but fixing on it as the focal point of the room, and let her mind wander. As she did, a look of worry settled over her features.

What worried her was violence. She sensed it coming to St. Denis just as she had sensed it that day in '42 when the German soldier had come to say a prayer at the grotto in the garden and she'd seen the blood dripping from his coat. St. Denis was a haven then, a showplace convent for well-to-do girls who sought solace from a world that seemed to have lost its mind. The killing and the war were someplace else, in small towns to the south and east whose names were easily forgotten. Here the bells rang out four times a day, morning vespers, meals, and evening prayers, just as they had for centuries. There were smiles, even occasional laughter.

Then they'd come, their thick boots crusted with mud, streaked with red, dragging their dead and wounded with them, right through the garden, killing the flowers. They set up a hospital in the name of the Reich, and that day the bells had stopped ringing.

Sister Marie-Thérèse had been no more than a wide-eyed novice then—a mere girl—and although she had felt the same shame and outrage the others felt when the Germans came, she did not understand the profound sense of loss Mother Superior must have felt when she acquiesced without so much as a word of protest.

She understood it now, however, and they were coming again, these storm troopers. They wore different uniforms, spoke a different language, but they were the same selfish, unholy men who intruded, defiled, stole peace in a world where peace was on the verge of extinction.

And it all centered on this new girl on the third floor.

Russian, they'd told her. Hah! From an aristocratic émigré family in Paris. This girl was no more an aristocrat than Joan of Arc. Sister Marie-Thérèse had known aristocrats when she was a girl, barons and baronesses, counts and countesses, and this girl had none of their sense of responsibility to the aristocracy. She was a bore, with her penchant for American cigarettes and her nervousness she tried so hard to disguise. She spoke French like a schoolgirl and Russian like a peasant.

And yet, all in all, it wasn't the girl who worried her. It was the men who'd preceded her.

Two of them in long tweed coats, the hair along their ears and necks badly cut. They had come the day before she arrived, keeping their hands in their pockets always, the way men will do when they have something to hide. They wanted to inspect the hospital, they said. They represented a wealthy industrialist who would be paying a visit and who would need the best accommodations, especially seclusion. They'd chosen St. Denis because of it. He was a German, this master of theirs, and under a great deal of pressure, but it wasn't German with which they mangled the tongue of holy St. Augustine. It was something more guttural, with origins further to the east.

One of them wore a gun under his coat. She'd seen it when he reached in to get a pad for making notes: a small, coal black gun that glinted in the sunlight. That was when she knew they were coming again, the killers who killed for money or country or some other false god, and she knew she could not fight them again. She was too old; she'd grown too accustomed to peace.

A pair of headlights swept the wall of the tiny chapel. Who could it be at this hour? she wondered. Then her old nun's heart began to beat wildly in her chest. It was them! The girl had been here less than a day, and they were here already! She grabbed the back of the pew with a gasp and tottered to her feet. She must stop them! She must bolt the door!

Cynthia Barnes watched the headlights break into a pattern and run across the wall. *Nick!* she thought excitedly.

She pulled on her robe and slid into the wheelchair. It was about time he'd got back. She had a list of complaints about this place as long as your arm, starting with that hoary old nun who badgered her night and day, and he was going to have to listen to every one of them.

She rolled to the window as the car stopped with a crunch on the gravel courtyard below. The sound gave her pause. It wasn't the sound made by a car making a leisurely call. There was an urgency in it she didn't like. It signaled danger.

Two sets of footsteps, one to the door, the other off down the drive. *Around to the back?* she thought. *Why is Nick sending someone around to cover the back?*

A second pair of headlights appeared on the wall as she heard the insistent knocking of the man at the door. Her heart leaped into her mouth. It wasn't Nick at all! The baited trap was being sprung *too soon*. Much too soon.

The nun at the door told the man to go away. Everyone was

sleeping. The man growled something in Russian, too indistinct to hear.

Cynthia rolled to the nightstand and picked up the pack of Benson & Hedges, pulled one out, and lit it. What was she to do? Wait?

The impossibility of successfully impersonating anyone's daughter suddenly came home to her, along with all she knew of Kobelev, his ruthlessness, his wild unpredictable temper. . . . The cigarette began to shake uncontrollably.

A soft rapping sounded at the door. "Mademoiselle, mademoiselle," came a woman's voice in a hoarse whisper.

"Who is it?"

"Sister Marie-Thérèse."

"Come in. Come in."

The old nun lumbered into the room. "They've come," she announced sternly.

"Who?"

"Whoever it is you're running from. They have caught up with you and you must go quietly. We cannot have any violence at the clinic. We have our other patients of which to think."

"Have I asked you for protection?" Cynthia asked coldly.

"No, you have not. But nevertheless, we want these men off the premises as soon as possible. I'll help you pack your things." She turned with the slow calculation of a battleship and began pulling clothes out of the dresser.

"You mean you'd hand me over to them even if you knew they had every intention of killing me?" Cynthia asked incredulously.

"That's no concern of mine or the clinic's. Our patients' outside lives are their own affair. There are times when even a sister of the Church must look the other way."

"Thanks a lot," mumbled Cynthia, snuffing out what was left of her cigarette.

The commotion at the front door had ceased. Now footsteps too numerous to count came tramping up the marble stairs toward the third floor.

"What if I told you they plan to kill me?"

The old woman stopped and stood still for a moment, a stack of underwear in her hand. "I would not want to know." She dropped the clothes, then bent and pulled out the lowest drawer.

"A man is with them. A Russian. A man who wants to be head of their secret police. He has killed a good many in his time, and I'm sure he won't hesitate to kill me either."

The woman stopped again, this time more briefly. "It is none of my concern," she said emphatically.

"I have friends who were going to protect me. They'll be back. You must tell them."

The old woman shook her head. "I cannot. You must not ask me."

The footsteps were in the hall.

"Dammit it, old woman, they didn't leave me a weapon."

The old nun threw the last of the clothes on the bed and glared down at Cynthia. Then her eyes softened and her lips pursed in a mass of wrinkles as though she were weighing something in her mind. A loud banging at the door made her jump.

"You're my only hope," Cynthia whispered as the old woman labored across the room to open it.

Two burly men pushed their way in, almost knocking the sister down. They wore identical black turtlenecks, and their heads had been shaved to an even stubble. One held a machine pistol on the old woman while the other quickly searched the room.

A few seconds later a third man came in and stood just inside the doorway. He was taller than the other two, his bearing more regal. His snow white hair was swept back off his forehead in a sharp widow's peak, and from beneath his arched brows his dark eyes darted, taking in everything at a glance.

Cynthia didn't need an introduction. The mad glint in those eyes was unmistakable. It could only be Nikolai Fedorovich Kobelev himself.

"Tatiana!" he exclaimed when those eyes finally lit upon her.

She tried to force a smile.

"I cannot let you take her," said the old nun, stepping forward.

"What?" asked Kobelev in French, turning to her in bemused amazement.

"She is a ward of the hospital. She must remain here until the doctor has signed her letters of discharge. I am sorry, but these are the rules."

"I don't care about your rules. This is my daughter."

"I am sorry, but I cannot allow it." She pushed herself between the goon with the gun and situated herself squarely between Kobelev and Cynthia. She was being foolish, thought Cynthia, but brave. "You have no right to barge in here and take one of my patients!" the old woman snapped. "We have procedures to follow and they simply cannot be ignored."

Kobelev snorted a short laugh, then turned to Cynthia. "Such is the security with which the Americans provide you," he said to her in Russian. Then he motioned to one of his men, who took the old woman forcibly by the arm and pulled her out of the way.

"You must not take her!" the old nun shouted, stamping her foot on the toe of the man who held her. He raised his foot in pain, and she pulled away and hobbled toward Kobelev. "In the name of the Church and all that is holy to man and God, I demand you leave these premises immediately!"

She reached him and grabbed him by the arm, although whether to restrain him or support herself was not altogether clear. Kobelev's eyes flashed angrily, and with a quick jerk of his head, he signaled the man with the gun. A short burst of gunfire and the nun collapsed against the bed.

"Sister!" Cynthia shouted mournfully, and Kobelev swung around to her wide-eyed. And in that brief instant the weeks of work by the team of plastic surgeons, the hours of studying films of Tatiana, the way she moved, tossed her head, held herself in her wheelchair, of memorizing every known fact of her background, and of imitating her voice until every intonation and nuance was honed to perfection, were lost. For that anguished moment, she was Cynthia Barnes, not Tatiana Kobelev.

FIVE

Carter peeked out from a darkened doorway in the headquarters of the *Freie Deutsche Jugend*, the Communist youth organization. The street was deserted in either direction except for a car parked against the opposite curb. Whether it was private or official was impossible to tell through the curtain of falling rain, but it was occupied. A trail of exhaust rose from its tailpipe.

So far he'd been lucky. In the two hours he'd spent in the Eastern Sector he'd encountered no one. Unlike its western counterpart, East Berlin is virtually deserted at night. Except for a few main thoroughfares, even the streetlights are turned off. He'd managed to walk the mile and a half to the Brandenburg Gate, slip in a side door, ascend the wrought-iron staircase to the roof, stash his cylinder, then slip away without being seen. The only person who might have noticed him, the guard stationed atop the gate to watch the wall, which was only a few hundred yards away, never stopped chewing his sandwich.

Now all that remained was to find Mariendorfstrasse, assess the security, then maybe get a few hours of sleep on a bench somewhere before the actual confrontation with Kobelev. According to Kliest, Mariendorfstrasse lay only two blocks north of his present position. He could walk it in a minute, except he had no wish to be seen, and his coal-stained clothes and blackened hands and face would certainly arouse suspicion.

A door opened in a building across the way, and an oblong of light spilled into the rain. Two men and a woman, singing a drinking song and laughing, staggered over to a car, pulled open its doors, and got in. Then the driver rolled the car into the center of the street, turned left, and disappeared. Carter waited until he heard them shifting into third in the next block before he pulled his coat collar up and started down the street.

No doubt a trap had been laid for him in Mariendorfstrasse. He expected it. He'd have lost respect for Kobelev if one hadn't. The trick was to reconnoiter early, figure a way to spring the trap without getting caught, and in the process get close enough to Kobelev to get off a shot.

It was a good bet Kobelev would show. If the information about his slipping prestige was accurate, it would mean he couldn't entrust killing Carter to a mere minion. He'd have to come himself to make sure the job was done right. And when he did show, Carter would kill him. This time there would be no mistake.

Mariendorfstrasse was dark, darker even than the other streets he'd passed through. It was after four-thirty by this time, and in other streets lights were coming on as people began to make ready to leave for work on the early shifts in the factories along Friedrichstrasse and Unter den Linden that opened at six. There were no such lights here, though. Here everything was black as ink.

Even the house numbers were invisible. If it weren't for the street sign at the corner indicating this was the unit block, he'd have no way of knowing where to find number fourteen. Carter assumed number one began on the south side and number two on the north as it did in most cities, and he began counting off the numbers as he walked.

There was something strangely quiet about this street. His footsteps sounded hollow against the pavement, and the houses themselves, which were little more than black outlines against the slightly grayer background of the night sky, seemed to float like ghost ships in a sea of black.

"Eight . . . ten," he counted, then his foot struck something on the sidewalk. He bent down. A stone or rather, as he examined it, a brick, broken in half. Odd, he thought, in a country that was normally so clean to find a broken brick lying out in the street. Then a trickling of realization began to pass through him, coupled with a premonition of disaster.

He ran to number fourteen. He got a few steps up the walk, then fell headlong into a pile of bricks and boards and chunks of plaster.

Bricks and boards and chunks of plaster—rubble! From his hands and knees he saw the house windows were nothing more than gaping holes with gray sky behind them.

Kobelev had tricked him! There was no safe house here. The whole street was nothing but a graveyard of bombed-out shells that hadn't been cleared since the end of World War II!

But why? Why send him on a wild-goose chase to East Berlin? To keep him out of the way while Kobelev ran an operation somewhere else? That had to be it. But where?

Dijon! The thought hit him with such certainty, he knew it had to be true. Somewhere there was a hole in the dam. Somehow, through some source no one had ferreted out yet, Kobelev had tumbled to where they were moving his "daughter," and he'd decided to snatch the bait before they could spring the trap. Security there wouldn't be battened down for another twenty-four hours. If he moved now, he could waltz in and waltz out without firing a shot.

Carter scrambled to his feet and started running, his mouth dry with fear. He had to get back as quickly as possible, because it wouldn't be long before Kobelev found out it wasn't Tatiana he'd snatched.

He rounded the corner into Friedrichstrasse, which was lit up like Fifth Avenue at Christmas, and flattened himself against a building. The city was starting to come alive. A few yards away a baker was unloading his truck, and at the next intersection cars were passing. He couldn't use the main thoroughfares any longer; he'd have to stick to the back streets and hope he wasn't seen.

He doubled back into Mariendorfstrasse and scaled a

mound of rubble between two of the houses. In the next street three houses had lights on, and in front of one a man was trying to grind a battered BMW to life. He cut between two houses that were still dark and started to scale a chain-link fence. He was poised on top of it, about to jump into the adjoining yard, when a fierce barking sent a jolt of adrenaline to his already racing heart.

He let himself down cautiously, pulling the Luger from its holster. The barking hushed to a low menacing growl. The dog was somewhere in the shadows, and although it was impossible to see it, the animal sounded big. Carter inched to his left, hoping to draw the beast into the light, but it held its ground.

As nearly as he could make out, he was in a narrow courtyard, the two long sides of which were brick walls. The ends, one leading to the alley and the other to the street, were fenced. The dog stood between him and the street end. He could always retreat the way he'd come, he thought, but there was no guarantee he wouldn't get half his leg torn off trying to climb the fence, and if he were going to have his pant leg and God-only-knew-what-else shredded, he might as well be going forward.

He began to move in that direction, hoping the low rumbling growl he was hearing was more threat than bite, when a light flashed on in a window overhead. The lock snapped open and someone began struggling to pull open the sash.

Carter dashed for the opposite fence. He'd mounted it and was about to pull his leg over when sharp teeth grabbed his ankle and wouldn't let go. By this time the window had been pulled open and the outline of a large woman loomed behind it. "*Wer ist da?*" she shouted.

Carter slammed the butt of the gun against the dog's head and the animal fell back.

Carter jumped and fell into a line of refuse containers that scattered and rolled, clanging in all directions. Another light snapped on in the house next door. He scrambled to his feet and began running headlong down the sidewalk.

A sharp pain in his left leg forced him to limp, slowing him down, but this didn't worry him particularly. In a few minutes that dog's owner would realize her pet was knocked out. Then the alarm would be raised and the border immediately closed. He had a plan for getting over the wall, but it depended on reaching Brandenburg and the cylinder before dawn. A police dragnet between here and the gate might hinder him considerably. His only hope, then, was to cover the ground before the police could mobilize to stop him.

He turned into Friedrichstrasse, this time heedless of the lights, passed the kiosks and empty shops, and headed for Unter den Linden, at the end of which was the Brandenburg Gate. He wondered if there were such things as joggers in East Germany. He must be quite a spectacle, he thought, limping along, his hands and face blackened with soot from the coal car, but he hadn't time to let it bother him.

The bus and truck traffic had greatly increased even in this short time, and private cars had begun to appear. The clock on the side of the Ministerium für Aussenhandel und Innerdeutschen Handel read five o'clock.

He reached Unter den Linden, the street Frederick the Great had hoped to turn into a showcase of the Prussian Empire by planting four rows of lime trees up its middle, and turned left. The leaves had all fled, and the lime trees looked like scrawny black hands clawing the night sky. He rushed off the curb just as a heavy, freight-laden truck rounded the corner. Its horn blared, and for an instant Carter froze in midstride, not knowing which way to jump. The eight huge back wheels clattered against the pavement as the driver tried to get it stopped. He couldn't and swerved, running the truck into a park bench and uprooting a tree.

Carter watched, slightly dazed, as clouds of steam rose from the truck's massive radiator and became lost in the gray mist. The driver's door opened, and a big man with his shirt-sleeves rolled tightly across his biceps climbed out.

"*Du . . .!* he began.

Carter took off again. Behind him someone shouted, "*Halten Sie!*" and a shot sounded. A second shot, and a white streak suddenly appeared on the pavement just in front of him. Up ahead Brandenburg loomed in the mist, not more than two blocks away.

A truck with a conveyor on its rear bumper churning a steady stream of vegetable crates into a store blocked the sidewalk just ahead. To go around meant swinging wide into the street and giving whoever was behind him a clear shot. Carter elected to go under and dove headfirst, but before he could pull himself up on the other side, a strong pair of hands grabbed his shoulders. He came up fighting, about to slam his fist into the man's belly, when the man quickly said, *"Ich bin ein Freund."* Their eyes met, and Carter made an instant decision to trust him.

He turned Carter forcibly around and shoved him toward a stack of empty crates in the alley just off the street. *"Hierin!"* he hissed.

Carter squeezed himself into a crate as tightly as he could, his cheeks resting on his knees, his breath coming in short rasping gasps.

The running footsteps came to a halt on the sidewalk a few feet away. "Where is he?" panted a voice in terse German.

"Around the corner, sir," said the vegetable vendor.

"You're lying!" shouted the policeman.

"No, sir. Please."

"You're hiding him."

"I'm telling you the truth, sir."

Carter noticed imprints of one bloody foot leading across the sidewalk to the front of the crate where he was hiding. He inched the Luger out of his coat to have it in hand in case the cop should look down.

"He went to the corner and turned!"

Carter listened while the cop made his decision, his heart beating in his throat. Then the footsteps began again, and Carter saw him in his dull gray uniform, his revolver drawn, head down the street, reach the corner, and disappear.

When he was gone, the vegetable vendor casually walked over and peered into the crate. His eyes fixed on the Luger, then on Carter. *"Uber die Wand?"* he asked.

Carter nodded. Yes, he was going over the wall.

"Also, gehen Sie!" With a jerk of his head he indicated Carter should get going.

Carter stood up and for an awkward moment wondered if he should thank the man. But the vendor seemed to have lost all interest in him. He'd turned his back and was throwing crates of cabbages onto a stack just inside the door.

Carter turned abruptly and ran down the wet pavement to the other end of the alley, paused to glance up and down the street, then went right toward the Brandenburg Gate.

The huge structure was clearly visible at the end of the block: a massive slab of mortar and marble held aloft by twelve stone columns bathed in spotlights. On the roof a statue of Peace drove four horses toward the heart of downtown Berlin.

He stopped by the cornerstone of a large building and surveyed the square. Nothing was moving. At the far end stood the Brandenburg Gate and beyond that the rolls of barbed wire marking the deathstrip that precedes the wall. Sirens sounded in the streets behind him not more than a few blocks away, and as he listened, he heard footsteps.

He sprinted across the open pavement, heedless of the pain in his leg. When he reached the side door of the gate's auxiliary building, he pressed himself tightly against the jamb and glanced back at the square. All was quiet. No sign of movement anywhere.

For a moment he stood there panting, thankful he'd made it this far and vowing to himself if he ever saw Kobelev again to make him pay heartily for this inconvenience. Then he tried the door.

He'd been this way earlier when he'd stashed the cylinder. He'd picked the lock, then when he'd returned, he'd jammed the bolt with a wadded piece of matchbook cover. As he pulled the knob now, it opened with only the slightest pressure. He slipped in and removed the cardboard wad to make sure the door locked behind him.

The room was pitch black except for a streak of light that shone out from under another door some twenty feet away.

This was the storage room for the historical museum that was attached to the gate. Carter crossed to the second door, opened it, then crossed behind the display cases of the museum proper, and started up a wrought-iron staircase that led up through the ceiling.

He had found this stairway earlier and knew that it led up to the roof. He also knew there was an observation post up there manned by a guard with a pair of binoculars who kept constant vigil on the wall. He'd had no trouble slipping past him the first time, but no doubt the man had been forewarned by now that a fugitive was in the area.

Carter ascended the stairs as silently as he could, and when he came to the heavy metal door at the top, opened it slowly. Through the crack he saw a bunker of sandbags with a machine gun in its center mounted on a tripod. A portable radio played strains of popular music, and a book lay propped open to someone's place. All the accouterments of habitation and no inhabitant. Where was the guard?

Carter opened the door a little wider. He was about to stick his head out when a violent jerk wrenched the doorknob from his hand and sent him sprawling headlong onto the roof. He looked up just in time to see a rifle butt rushing for his face. He turned and it smashed against the tiles inches from his ear. The soldier reared back for another try, but Carter drove his left fist into the soft putty of the man's face. His nose broke with a gush and he dropped the rifle. Carter then buckled his legs against the man's chest and sprung, flinging him backward. His head hit the metal door with a dull clang, and he fell forward, dazed but not unconscious.

Carter was on him in a second. He drew out the Luger and clipped him on the base of the skull. Then he spun around to make sure there weren't any more of them.

He dragged the guard's body over against the sandbags and peered down into the street. Two military vehicles were converging on Checkpoint Charlie, which was located directly in front of the Brandenburg Gate. At the checkpoint six or seven soldiers with submachine guns strapped to their backs stood in the dim light of the guard's booth, talking.

Overhead the sky was a stolid gray just charged now with the first light of dawn. Carter studied the sky with disquietude. It was now or never.

He pulled out his cylinder from where he'd stashed it under the chariot of the huge statue and brought it to the edge of the roof. On his hands and knees he unzipped the casing and stripped it off. Then he laid out the long sheets of nylon tenting and began to fit in the thin metal rods that he had placed at the cylinder's core. In a few minutes the construction was complete: a single, twelve-foot-long, batlike wing with an aluminum frame underneath to which to secure himself—a hang glider as complete and controllable as any that ever graced the sunny coastline of California, only as portable as an umbrella.

His sole piece of good fortune lay in the fact that the wind was blowing from east to west—over the wall. He carried his contraption to the edge and after some preliminary testing, entrusted himself to the air. The left wing dipped dangerously, and for a moment he thought he would fall, but then the updraft in front of the massive gate caught him and buoyed him skyward.

His heart fluttered with the thrill of flight. The ground below, the military sedans that were now disgorging more troops in front of the checkpoint, the men already there sniffing the air for his scent like hounds, machine guns at the ready, all slipped silently by as he sailed unnoticed into West Berlin.

SIX

Once on the ground Carter went straight to Kliest's, retrieved his bag, showered, and on a phone Kliest assured him was clean, placed a call to Hawk. It was after midnight on the East Coast, but Hawk answered on the first ring.

"We got a nasty little missive from Kobelev earlier tonight," Hawk said after he'd answered Carter's initial barrage of questions and confirmed his worst fears about what had happened to Cynthia. "Apparently he's holding the girl aboard the Orient Express. He says he wants his daughter and you turned over to him, or he'll kill her. We've got until the train reaches Istanbul to make our decision."

"Have the railroad authorities been contacted? What about the local police?"

"They're all willing to cooperate fully. We had a little trouble to begin with, but a phone call from the head of State to each of the countries involved soon straightened everything out. A little presidential muscle can work wonders. At any rate, it seems Kobelev's commandeered the train. He's not letting anyone off or on, although he's allowing the train to make its scheduled stops. It's either that or snafu rail traffic over the whole of Europe."

"How do I get aboard?"

"That's something you'll have to work out with Leonard Southby. He's the owner of the train. I've arranged for you to meet with him in the bar of the Sacher Hotel in Vienna this afternoon at two. When I talked to him earlier tonight he was ready to mobilize NATO to get his train back. It took a lot of convincing to get him to let us handle it our way. I'm afraid if he hangs around that bar too long he'll start talking nuclear war again and won't be in any shape to help us."

"Yes, sir."

"By the way, Nick, I'm sorry for this little setback. And that's what it is, a setback. Let's not kid ourselves."

An admission of error was a rare thing from Hawk. It bespoke the gravity of the situation, and Carter treated it with the care it deserved.

"I'm sure this is going to work out."

"Perhaps. Perhaps not. In any event our initial goal has been met. Kobelev has come out from behind his curtain of security. He's accessible now and we can still take him."

"Yes, sir."

"The man has to be taken, N3. Has to, no matter what the cost."

"I understand that, sir."

Before Hawk rang off, the two men worked out some of the logistics Carter would need over the next few days. Hawk provided a list of AXE operatives in cities along the train's route and the number Carter could call in Washington should he run into trouble. They agreed that Vienna was a good choice for boarding the train as it was only half an hour by jet from Berlin and would allow Carter a few hours' rest at Kliest's before going on.

Then, when all the business had been conducted and there was nothing left to say, Hawk lingered a moment on his end of the line. "Take care of yourself," he said finally.

Carter sensed he meant it. "I will. Thank you, sir."

Kliest, who had been sitting on the edge of his armchair listening to Carter's end of the conversation, abruptly stood and went into the kitchen area. When he returned he was carrying a tray piled high with German pancakes, sausages, and a liter stein of rich beer. "My wife made these up before she went to work. They've been in the oven warming. I'll make up the bed while you're eating."

• • •

Carter ate, made his travel arrangements, and slept. In a few hours Kliest woke him and drove him to the airport. As he was boarding his plane, Kliest gave his hand a firm shake and told him it had been a pleasure working with him. Between Kliest's sendoff and Hawk's good-bye over the phone, Carter wondered if anyone really expected him to come back from this assignment alive.

In Vienna he deplaned, stored his luggage, and caught a cab for the Sacher Hotel. Leonard Southby was at the bar hunched over a glass of scotch. Sitting next to him was a small man wearing large glasses.

"Mr. Welter," Southby said, introducing him after Carter sat down, "from our public relations department." Carter noticed the glasses achieved a friendly effect by being a shade too small to be considered comical.

Welter nodded brusquely. The glasses were friendly; Welter definitely was not.

"I'm not happy, Mr. Carter," Southby went on, motioning to the bartender to bring Carter a drink and freshen his own. "You're better than the combined police forces of France, Germany, Austria, Hungary, Yugoslavia, and Bulgaria because you're going to do the impossible. You're going to get my train back."

"Sometimes one man can do what many can't," said Carter. "As for getting your train back, let's put it this way. You and I both have an interest in seeing Nikolai Kobelev removed from the picture."

"Did you hear that, Sidney?" Southby asked in a loud voice, turning to Welter. "We have a mutual interest, Mr. Carter and I. A ten-million-dollar train at stake, not to mention the lives of a hundred and fifty fare-paying patrons for whom I am legally responsible, and Mr. Carter wants to talk about our mutual interest. Go away, Mr. Carter," he said angrily, turning back around. "I'm not interested in a man whose interests don't coincide exactly with mine. I don't trust a government stooge. You people are always looking to protect your precious state secrets. I buy and sell your kind all the time. I want a man on my payroll who will do exactly as I tell him."

Carter calmly swished the ice in his drink and laid the swizzle stick on the bar. "I'm afraid you're stuck with me."

"I am not stuck, sir! I may be tired, overwrought, even half-drunk, but I am not stuck. We have ways of dealing with this kind of terrorism in Europe—men trained by the terrorists themselves who are enlightened enough to realize money is more important than ideals. I can afford to buy several of these men and have the OE back on schedule before she reaches Belgrade."

Carter took a close look at Southby over the rim of his glass. The man was obviously on the brink of nervous exhaustion. "Apparently they didn't tell you who we're dealing with," he said, putting his drink back on the bar. "Nikolai Kobelev is no ordinary terrorist. He's Russian. KGB. The men around him are all handpicked, I'm sure. Efficient killers, each one of them. Handling this sort takes a certain talent, shall we say, a talent you can't buy, Mr. Southby, at any price. I don't think Kobelev is interested in your train as such. It merely provides a means to greater ends, namely to recover his daughter—who is in our custody—and to give him the opportunity to wreak vengeance on me. He will take your train to Istanbul, where he has no doubt made additional arrangements for his transportation into Russia, then leave it. On the other hand, if it suits his purpose to blow up your ten-million-dollar toy, he will do so without a moment's hesitation. If Kobelev manages to recover his daughter and eliminate me, he will have gone a long way toward capturing what he really wants."

Southby's stern expression softened. Like many a man who has spent hours in a bar wallowing in his trouble, his moods changed rapidly from anger to maudlin self-pity. "I'm sorry, Mr. Carter, truly I am, but the Orient Express is my life. When I first bought her she was a broken-down rusted mess, headed for the scrapyards. I reclaimed her from oblivion. I painstakingly restored every inch of her, put new leather on her seats, new drapes; I hired the finest woodcrafters in Europe to repair her interior. There are no new cars on that train. She's exactly as she was in 1929 in her heyday. I put a fortune into her and built a fortune with her.

She's my baby."

"All this is very touching," said Carter dryly, "but beside the point. What I need from you, Southby, is a way to board her without being immediately recognized."

Southby quickly drained his drink and put his glass on the bar with a heavy sigh. "Welter and I have discussed that," he said. "Vienna is a dinner stop. We thought there might be some way to poison the food."

"Highly unlikely," said Carter, "unless you want to poison everyone on the train and they all start eating at exactly the same moment. But what do you mean by dinner stop? I thought there were dining cars."

"There are. You see, the Orient Express isn't a passenger train as such anymore, in the sense that people get on and off at different stops. It's a package tour. You buy a ticket in Paris and ride all the way through to Istanbul. Of course, there are extras along the way. Tonight was supposed to have been dinner here at the hotel for all the passengers, then an evening at the opera. Naturally, in view of recent developments, all this was canceled. But we've contacted Wagon Lits, who does our catering, and they've consented to send down one of their chefs from the Paris office. We have to keep up appearances. We've arranged to have him board here and cook a gourmet meal right on the train."

"And Kobelev is going along with this?"

"Oh, he's been very accommodating. Said he'd be perfectly willing to let us wine and dine him in the best style Europe has to offer if that's what we want."

"I can imagine. This chef, when does he arrive?"

"He's here now, at our branch office. He's due to board at four."

"Call him. Tell him he can go back to Paris. I'll be taking his place tonight."

"If you insist." Welter put a commiserating arm around Southby's shoulder.

"Don't worry about a thing," said Carter.

Southby groaned.

Carter found the chef, a rotund, genial little man, sitting in a straight-backed chair in the front office of Special Tours, Inc., a black overcoat draped over his shoulders and a battered suitcase at his feet. He told Carter he'd been ordered home, a circumstance to which he seemed resigned, as though his world consisted of contradictory orders to do one thing, then to turn around and do the opposite with no explanation whatever.

From him Carter learned things the tour staff had known from the beginning but which had never penetrated the upper echelons of management. The train engineer, for example, belonged to several Communist Party organizations in Paris; and the night before, when Kobelev had flagged the train at a crossing outside Dijon, it was thought the engineer was in league with them. He had since disappeared, and one of Kobelev's men was running the train. Carter made a mental note to have the man picked up and questioned.

He learned, too, that Cynthia was still in the wheelchair, and when she boarded the night before, she'd seemed dazed or drunk. Carter assumed drugs. The chef had heard this from the woman in the office who had been in radio contact with the train before the Russians had commandeered all communications aboard. Carter added another note to talk with her before he left.

The chef went on to say that Cynthia was being guarded by Kobelev and two of his men in the salon car, which was in the middle of the train, and that four others, two with machine guns, were circulating among the other passengers. This meant eight Russians in all, including the man at the controls.

When he felt he'd found out all he could from the chef, Carter excused himself, went outside, and ducked into a small bistro down the street. He purchased a bottle of cognac and two glasses. When he returned he and the chef toasted one another's health and the health of President Mitterand and most of the French parliament before the chef had to leave for the train station to make his connection for Paris. Before he left, the chef thanked him effusively, and Carter made him a present of the rest of the bottle.

Carter watched the taxi round the corner out of sight, then he went in to talk with the woman behind the desk. It was she who had talked with the train staff by radio, and although her distaste for the Russians and what they'd done was admirable, she wasn't able to add anything to what the chef had already told him. Finally she said that if he were going to be a chef, he'd need a uniform, and she gave him the address of a store in Schillerstrasse.

The store's tailor turned out to be tight-lipped and efficient, like most German professional people; a slash of chalk along the sleeve and another across the front sufficed for altering the jacket, but the trousers were another matter. Carter took the man aside and explained his rather special problem.

He held out the Luger in its leather holster, which was shiny from constant handling. "Normally, you see, I wear her under here." He held the holster up under his arm. "But I can rig the straps around my waist, like this." He put the holster on like a belt and turned the gun until it rested in the small of his back. "This makes it more difficult for them to find in a search. What I need, then, is a little extra give in the pants to cover it. Maybe an insert or two."

The tailor nodded and quickly took some measurements of the gun and of Carter's waist with the gun in place. Then he left, and Carter took a chair in the front of the shop and began reading the Viennese daily he found lying across it.

There was nothing in the newspaper about the train or the kidnapping, and this pleased him. Apparently the authorities were cooperating as Hawk had said.

In less than an hour the uniform was ready. Carter tried it on, and the jacket and pants fit perfectly. Even Wilhelmina was snug and virtually undetectable in a V-shaped pouch at his back. A white chef's hat and he could easily have passed for a Cordon Bleu graduate.

He thanked the tailor and told him to wrap the uniform. Then he dressed again in his street clothes, gathered up the packages, and left. On the way back to the tour office he bought a secondhand leather suitcase covered with stickers from European resort cities.

He put the uniform on in a small washroom in the rear of the tour office, then pulled all the American labels out of his clothes and packed them in the old suitcase. Then he put on the chef's hat and looked at himself in the mirror.

He felt vaguely ridiculous, but that was to be expected. The big question was: would he be recognized? Kobelev would know him immediately, of course, having met him before, but he was fairly certain Kobelev would not be doing the preliminary inspection. According to the chef, members of the train's staff who had put in twice their normal shift had been allowed off in Salzburg and replacements allowed to board (which gave one some indication of the importance Kobelev placed on his personal comfort). These replacements had been given only the most cursory going-over by a big Russian guard whom the chef had described ("*Grand, monsieur, très grand*. As beeg as le grand Charles himself. Beegair.") and whom Carter was certain he'd never seen. All this assumed, of course, that this guard—whoever he was—had never seen Carter's photograph, and while Carter made it a point of professional caution never to have pictures taken, it was always a risky business betting what Russian intelligence did or did not let its underlings know and see.

At any rate, he felt he didn't need any more of a foothold than mere access to the train. Once on, he'd find Kobelev and do what he had to do.

As he stared at his reflection, a number of things went through his mind, including the fact that Kobelev was by far the most able adversary he'd ever faced. For a moment the thought made him uneasy. But then he felt Hugo strapped to his arm, Wilhelmina against the small of his back, and Pierre in its pouch high on his thigh, and there was solace in knowing they were close at hand.

After all, he was well-trained. Hawk saw to that. Refresher courses every six months in small arms and antipersonnel technology, not to mention constant workouts to keep himself in peak physical condition. And his instincts, too, honed by invaluable experience—a million refinements of the agent's art accomplished by years of grinding daily routine. He was, in short, the best the American side had to offer.

Unfortunately, he thought, as he packed up the suitcase

where it lay across the toilet seat, Kobelev was the best their side had as well.

Outside, the woman behind the desk excitedly told him about a piece of luck she'd had locating suitable identification. One of the porters had lost his passport on board, and it had been found by a maintenance man and left in the office. It even had a card from the French caterer's union. Of course, she said, only a myopic customs official on a foggy day would ever think the man in the photograph and Carter were one and the same, but still it provided something for him to flash in case he was asked.

Carter, who carried his own false papers, could not bring himself to disappoint her. He thanked her with a tip of his chef's hat and stuffed the passport in the breast pocket of his jacket. Then he said good-bye and strode out the door.

Two blocks away in front of the Osterreicher Hotel he caught a cab and told the driver to take him to the headquarters of the Viennese police. The driver turned into Goethestrasse, jerked to a halt in front of a gargoyle-encrusted building. Carter got out of the cab and went in.

At the front desk he identified himself as the American agent come to handle the kidnapped train. He was immediately ushered in to see the superintendent who turned out to be a small balding man with a Prussian mustache. The police chief studied his papers, then tossed them back across the desk. He said he assumed Carter was in disguise and had not come to cook him dinner.

Carter assured him he would make no attempt to take over the train while on Viennese soil, and the superintendent asked if he could extend that to include all of Austria and not move against the Russians until the train reached the Austro-Hungarian border sometime the following morning. After all, he explained, the Russians still enjoyed favorable relations with the Hungarians, and one must live with one's neighbors, wasn't that so? His friends in State Security would appreciate it.

Carter agreed to the superintendent's request, even though in truth he hadn't the vaguest idea of what he was going to do once on board. The superintendent then made a call and when he hung up, told Carter he was cleared to board the train whenever he wished. Carter thanked him and left.

Surprisingly, the train was not surrounded by police barricades and crowds of onlookers as Carter had expected. The entire fifteen cars of the Orient Express, including its gleaming black antique steam engine, rested on a side track in a far corner of the rail yard awaiting the time it could resume its scheduled place in the scheme of European rail traffic, and although movement was visible behind the dusty car windows, the area around the train seemed deserted. All the same, as he made his way across the tracks, he had the feeling he was being watched.

The feeling was confirmed when a door opened in a small weathered shack nearby and a policeman wearing the typical Austrian helmet, similar to those worn by the Kaiser's army in World War I, came out to intercept him. "Who are you?" he asked in German.

"The chef," Carter replied. He didn't know if the cop had been informed of what was happening or not.

"Your papers."

Carter handed him the passport the woman in the tour office had given him. The man studied it, shook his head, and gave it back. "I don't know who you people think you're fooling," he said with disgust. "Special forces. Secrecy. Nonsense, if you ask me. Hit them hard and fast. That's the way we would have done it in the old days."

Carter nodded and grunted and shoved the porter's passport back into the pocket of his jacket and continued his solitary way to the train.

He chose a middle car, threw his bag to the top of the boarding ladder, and was about to climb up when a snub-nosed revolver appeared out of the darkness at the top of the stairs. The barrel looked to be the size of a bazooka. Carter raised his hands and backed off.

As the hand holding the gun emerged from the gloom and became an arm, then a shoulder, Carter's eyes widened and his mouth dropped open. Coming toward him was one of the largest, most simianlike men Carter had ever seen: head as large as a bowling ball, covered with short black hair and looking about as impenetrable; forehead of an ape, only inches from widow's peak to bushy brows and yet two handspans across, framing a lantern-jawed face in which each feature was grossly outsize, including huge lips that ill concealed a set of broken, ragged-looking teeth. And yet, big as it was, the head was too small for the body. An enormous physique stuffed into clothes that looked as though he'd swum in them, let them dry in place, and they'd shrunk several sizes. Biceps, deltoid, and pectoral muscles threatened to burst every seam. Carter assailed the man first in German, then in French, neither of which seemed to have any effect. The monster only grunted several times and motioned with his gun for Carter to raise his hands even higher.

Then his huge hands reached out and began groping Carter's clothes. Carter held his breath while large fingers closed almost completely around biceps and thighs. He felt them on his legs and shoulders, even his ankles, but they missed by some miracle the V-shaped pouch at the small of his back where Wilhelmina lay hidden.

The man stood, looking down with beady, dull eyes from about the same height as an adult looks down on a child, and jerked his head in the direction of the train.

Carter saw no reason to wait to be asked twice. He climbed hastily up the stairs, opened the door, and went inside.

As it turned out, he'd found the rear of the dining car on the first try. The assistant chef and two waiters, who were standing and talking in a gleaming white, although very compact kitchen, looked at him when he came in, their eyes registering puzzlement and fear. Partly because they had no idea who he was, thought Carter, and partly because after all that had happened in the last sixteen hours, they'd come to fear everything.

SEVEN

Although Nick was considered, among some of his friends, to be a pretty fair gourmet cook, he had never prepared a meal for such a large group before. The situation was further complicated by the presence of Vasili Shurin (which Carter soon learned was the Russian giant's name).

He stood like a huge piece of misplaced furniture at the end of one of the preparation counters, hands behind his back, grinning a ragged-toothed idiotic grin, blocking the flow of traffic so that whenever a tray of dishes or a pan of food needed transportation from one end of the narrow kitchen to the other, the transporter had to yell to Shurin to stand back, a situation made even more difficult by the fact that the man understood neither French nor German, and his Russian vocabulary seemed to be limited to the simplest words. Still he stood, smiling moronically and nodding in a mockery of understanding whenever spoken to, and watched pop-eyed as each new ingredient was added to the main dishes.

Fortunately, Carter had arrived late, and the assistant chef had taken it upon himself to prepare *coq au vin* casseroles in case the chef were delayed or unable to board for some reason. It was upon this contingency that they now fell back, fixing the accompanying French-cut string beans almondine and thin, buttered noodles, and crepes filled with puréed chestnuts for dessert—all in all, an admirable dinner, although Carter was able to convince the assistant chef to sabotage it in small ways to keep Kobelev from sending for the chef to thank him in person.

As far as the actual cooking, Carter's role consisted of running back and forth tasting and clucking his tongue and watching others do the work, mostly for Shurin's benefit, and cornering each waiter, porter, and anyone else who had been outside the kitchen to learn as much about the layout of the train and the habits of the guards as he could.

The salon car where Cynthia was being held was the second car forward from the dining car. In between was a club car with a small bar and some additional seating for diners. At the bar sat a hatchet-faced man with a submachine gun on his knees. The weapon seemed to be a physical part of him; no one had seen him put it down, even to eat.

The salon car itself consisted of another small bar, some swivel chairs, tables, and a piano. A guard stood at either door and allowed entrance to no one, not even to the waiter with the dinner cart, so what was going on inside—what condition Cynthia might be in, and the mood of Kobelev—was unknown.

After Carter had learned everything he could, he decided to do a little exploring on his own. Swearing loudly in French, which startled everyone, he said he'd forgotten some indispensable, very special ingredient for the beans almondine. Begging his pardon, he squeezed past Shurin and slipped into the storage area at the back of the car. He watched for a moment to make sure Shurin was occupied elsewhere, then opened the rear door and stepped out into the narrow enclosure over the coupling between the cars.

Here the smell of exhaust and engine oil was strong. On either side was a hinged half door that opened inward. Carter opened it, stuck out his head, and looked up and down the track. Southby had not exaggerated about the age of the cars. A narrow ladder ran up the side to the roof of each of them, as it did on most passenger cars before the advent of streamlining and as it still did on freight cars.

Carter closed the door and went back inside. In the roof of the kitchen was a small square portal for ventilation such as were used before air conditioning. Through the pass-through he could see there was one in the dining area as well.

His mind began to churn, formulating a plan, as he walked toward the front of the kitchen. He'd turned sideways and was slipping between Shurin's enormous chest and the counter when Wilhelmina knocked against the Formica with a metallic clunk. Anxiously Carter looked up to see if Shurin had heard, but the little apelike eyes were fixed on the other end of the car where the assistant chef was checking on the chicken.

Safe this time, thought Carter as he slipped through and nodded an "excuse me," but it was always a dangerous business banking on another man's stupidity. From now on he'd have to be more careful.

Early dinner service ended at eight o'clock. At nine-fifteen a heavy jolt signaled the train had begun to move again. At the back of the kitchen, where clean-up was just ending, everyone was apprehensive. They wondered where they were going and how it would all end now that this trouble had thrust itself upon them. Ultimately, each pair of eyes fell upon Carter, who could do no more than shrug impatiently and move off down the aisle toward the refrigerators.

Steam from the cooking and dishwashing hung in the air, and coats, which had been removed, were slow to be replaced. The small area soon seemed full of red suspenders and T-shirts, all but Carter's portion of it, whose jacket, much whiter than the others, remained where it was.

Shurin, too, stood off to one side, separated from the others by a gulf of language and circumstance, the outsider who seemed to want to join in so much, whose face wore a permanent silly, childish smile, fun-loving and stupid. He'd been the butt of occasional jokes while the men were working, never to his face, of course, and never in Russian, but good-naturedly, as though some zookeeper had stopped by and dropped off a potentially dangerous but playful great ape for everyone to enjoy.

Only he wasn't smiling now. His lips were compressed and thoughtful, and his eyes rather cold as he stared at Carter. "Take off your coat," he said in Russian. His voice was calm, but Carter sensed it was the calm before a storm.

The master chef pretended he hadn't heard.

"Remove your coat," Shurin said again, louder and this time in halting French.

The sound of the big man speaking French caused everyone to stop and look at him. Eyes went from Shurin to Carter and instinctively every man in the room shrunk back as far as he was able in the narrow confines, opening a path between the two.

For a moment no one said anything. The only sound was the clack of the wheels and the creaking of the old car as the train made its slow way out of the station. To Carter it seemed as though someone had suddenly turned up the heat. Beads of sweat sprouted on his forehead.

"What?" he asked, unable to come up with anything better.

"You have something under your coat. Remove it." The little eyes bore down on him like two shiny black beads set in dough.

Carter began slowly to unbutton his chef's jacket, desperately trying to think of a way he could slip his hand around and draw the Luger.

As he watched, the big man cautiously pulled out his massive revolver.

Carter now had all the buttons undone and the jacket thrown back on his shoulders. When he let it fall, the holster strap around his waist would be visible.

"Drop it," the big man said, walking forward, the gun in his hand. He came to within an arm's length of Carter when the train passed over the switch that separated the side track from the main line, and the car rolled violently to one side, throwing him off balance.

Carter seized the opportunity. He reared back and kicked him squarely in the crotch. The heavy brows and massive mouth contorted in an expression of absolute pain, and the big gun hit the floor.

Carter started to pull Wilhelmina from her holster when the safety caught for a split second on a thread the tailor had neglected to snip, slowing the movement by a fraction of a second and giving the big Russian, who was quickly recovering, enough time to paw the gun out of his hand and send it crashing into the stove front half the car away.

Carter sought the advantage by backhanding the man across the face. It had no effect. Shurin merely stared at him, blinking.

Carter swung again, a hard right to the cheek. And again Shurin stared, the anger slowly starting to build in him like steam in a boiler.

Desperate now, Carter hit him again on the jaw, then the cheeks, throwing all his weight behind it. But it was like hitting thinly padded rock. Shurin didn't even try to defend himself. His huge hands hung at his sides, his thick fingers twitching with rage.

Carter hammered at the man, his arms working like pistons, until the big Russian lunged like a bull, making a grab for Carter's head. Carter neatly skipped back a step, and the big man missed, stumbled, and almost fell on his face, saving himself at the last minute by catching the edge of the counter.

Carter needed maneuvering room, but in the narrow kitchen there wasn't any. He'd already stepped into a blind alley of cabinets and refrigeration units, and as Shurin pulled himself to his feet, his massive body blocked the only avenue of escape.

Shurin saw that he had his quarry trapped, and his thick lips parted in a leer as he came forward, closing the gap on Carter.

Carter retreated, his hands groping desperately for something to throw. They lit upon a rack of heavy iron skillets. He unhooked the first in line and slung it. It landed with a dull metallic ring against Shurin's upraised arms and thudded to the floor. Carter followed with a second, third, and fourth skillet, eventually emptying the entire rack. All of them bounced harmlessly off Shurin the way Carter remembered bullets used to bounce off Superman.

Carter was running out of options. The waiters and cooks all looked on, too dumbfounded to do anything. Then Carter felt the cold steel of the cooler door against his back and knew he'd backpedaled as far as he could. He'd have to stand and fight.

Shurin waded in the way a rude man might enter a crowded room, arms out in front of him, face turned slightly to one side as Carter continued to rain punches on him, although by this time the blows were losing some of their conviction.

When he got close, Shurin stooped down until he and Carter were nose to nose, then he wrapped his arms around the smaller man like a big Russian bear. The great vise of muscle and sinew began to squeeze shut. A sickening crunch erupted from Carter's rib cage and it became impossible to breathe.

Carter looked wildly around for help, but there was nothing the other men could do but stand and gape.

Then a burst of pain went off like an alarm in the middle of his back. The Russian was wedging his thumbs between two vertebrae. Another few seconds and he'd split them, snapping Carter's back like a chicken bone.

Quickly Carter shook his sleeve, and Hugo slipped into his hand. Then blindly he thrust the stiletto into the big man's left side, like Ahab jabbing his harpoon into the whale, again and again, searching for the heart.

Shurin stumbled back against an open spice rack, sending jars and cans flying in all directions, but he righted himself almost immediately, never losing his grip.

At first Carter's desperation and the enormous pain prevented him from concentrating, and his knife blows went wild. He hit the stomach, the side, the bicep, the back, but nothing he did would release the steellike pincers in which he'd gotten caught. He desperately needed one deep breath. Then by sheer willpower he brought himself under control. He ran the blade point down the xylophone of the man's rib cage, found the soft section even through his clothes, stood the knife on point, and jammed it in with the heel of his hand.

The arms suddenly released like fingers around something hot, and Carter slumped to the floor, gasping.

Shurin tottered back against the counter, his back and

side soaked in blood. He managed to get the knife blade out, looked at it dumbly, then he pitched forward like a fallen tree, headfirst onto the floor.

When he fell it was as though an orchestra had reached a great crashing crescendo. After the last echo died, the audience of cooks and waiters suddenly sprang to life.

"*Mon Dieu!* Monsieur, we did not think you would live," exclaimed the assistant chef as they ran to help Carter up.

Carter staggered to his feet, holding on to a cabinet with one hand and grasping his side with the other. Air rushed into his lungs like a hot gas, causing agonizing pain. Every rib felt broken.

He pointed to the body. "Get him out of here," he croaked hoarsely. "Throw him off the train."

One of the waiters folded Shurin's thick arms across his chest; then with the help of three others, he dragged him out the back door by his trouser cuffs.

"Where's my gun?" asked Carter. The assistant chef fetched it from the front of the car and handed it to him. Carter stuffed it back in his holster. "Nothing's happened here. If anybody asks, Shurin is gone. Same goes for me. I'm in one of the parlor cars in back. Someone is going to have to clean up all this blood."

"We'll take care of it, monsieur. But monsieur—you don't look well. Your face is pale. Please, sit down and rest." The assistant chef tried to take his arm.

"I'll be all right," said Carter, pulling away. "I've got unfinished business up front." Hobbling with pain, he went out the door into the narrow passageway at the car's rear. The assistant chef followed anxiously. In the passageway Carter pulled open the half door and with a great deal of difficulty managed to mount himself on its edge with one foot outside the train.

"Isn't this a bit foolhardy in your condition?" asked the chef.

"Don't worry about me!"

"Very well, monsieur."

"And remember, if they question you, you didn't see this,

and you and your men know nothing about Shurin's whereabouts. These Russian guards sometimes have funny ideas about revenge."

"Yes, monsieur."

Carter pulled himself onto the ladder and began climbing. The rain and overcast had broken up, and the moonlight clearly lit the Alps towering around him. A valley stretched out below for a dizzying distance.

When he reached the top he lay down flat on his back, gasping. He hadn't intended to try this until later when everyone was asleep, but Shurin had forced his hand. He had to make his move now before the man was missed.

He pulled himself to his feet, ran a few yards along the roof of the car, then stopped, unable to go any further. His ribs were on fire. Every movement was torture. It felt as though the giant's arms were still around him. And yet he had to go on.

He reached the end of the dining car and jumped to the salon car. He landed badly, trying to roll to absorb the shock and rolling right on his rib cage. He lay for several seconds, fighting to stay conscious in spite of the enormous swell of pain from his sides. Finally it began to subside, and he was able to sit up and pull himself into a crouching position.

He clambered across the top of the club car, but this time, instead of jumping, he tried to step onto the salon car. Unfortunately, the cars were swaying at an opposite rhythm, and as he stood with one foot on either car, the movement threatened to topple him backward off the mountainside. For a moment it looked as though he'd made a fatal error, but he managed to grab hold of the small wheel that operated the car's manual brake and pull himself on board.

Both vent holes, fore and aft, were clearly visible in the car's roof. Carter wondered which would be the most advantageous for his entrance. He would have to take one guard out with his first shot, which meant with the other it would probably degenerate into a gun battle. If he chose the near vent, there might be time for the guard in the club car to get in and catch him in a crossfire. The next car up was a sleeping car, and according to his information there was no guard in this, so he opted for the far vent.

He made his way across the car's roof as stealthily as he could, lifted the lid on the vent, and peeked in. No one was there. He crouched to get a better angle. Kobelev sat in a swivel chair in a booth by the bar, looking directly at him, a revolver to Cynthia's temple. Instinctively Carter drew back—and the back of his head hit the hard metal of a gun barrel.

"Won't you come in, Mr. Carter?" shouted Kobelev from the car below. "We've been expecting you."

EIGHT

Tatiana Kobelev reached across the narrow bed table and picked a card off the pile. A triumphant grin lit her face. "Gin!" she announced, laying her cards out.

The old nurse sighed and threw down her hand. She started to say something, then apparently thought better of it, and resignedly began to gather the cards into a deck.

"I think I like this American game," Tatiana said.

"It's more fun when you don't cheat," the old nurse said sourly.

"I do not cheat! How dare you accuse me of cheating?"

"The proof is right here," said the nurse, coming around to the bed and fumbling beneath the blanket next to Tatiana. Tatiana tried to stop her, but the old woman managed to grab the queen of hearts and hold it up to her. "You see? You picked up two cards on the last turn and stashed the extra here. Do you think I'm a fool?"

"No! I think you are a peasant strumpet and a whore!" Tatiana shouted at the top of her voice.

The old woman's eyes narrowed and her face trembled with anger. Suddenly she lashed out and slapped the Russian girl's cheek.

"Whore! Whore! Whore!" the girl chanted.

A Marine stuck his head in at the door. "Everything all right in here, Lieutenant Dilsey?"

The old nurse sighed. "Missy here's just feeling her oats, is all."

"Why don't you come out of there for a while, ma'am? Give yourself a break. You remember what happened to Lieutenant Green."

"Sergeant, I don't have to be reminded what happened to the girl's previous nurse. I have no intention of letting this young lady get under my skin like that. Besides, she is not supposed to be left without supervision."

"I know that, ma'am, but a few minutes won't hurt. You haven't had a break from this for over a week."

"Two weeks."

"Exactly, ma'am."

"All right. My replacement will be here shortly anyway. And you're certainly not going anywhere, are you, dearie?"

Tatiana stared up at her sullenly, pure hate in her eyes.

The old woman stared back unflinchingly, then turned and left, locking the door behind her.

The room fell suddenly silent, except for the rush of air in the heating vent. For a moment Tatiana looked around, savoring her solitude. She'd been left to herself precious few times since coming to this awful place, and when one of these rare moments chanced to happen, it was not to be squandered wantonly.

She threw off the blanket, swung her feet out, and let herself down on the floor. Then using the bed table and the edge of the mattress for support, she pushed herself upright. She let go of the table and bed, and for one wavering, unsteady moment, was alone on the floor. Then she lost her balance and had to grab the bed to keep from falling.

Yes, she was doing nicely. With a few minutes' practice, the simple movements of walking and standing would come back to her. The exercises at night were paying off. The muscles were strong; they'd simply forgotten what to do.

She inched her way toward the foot of the bed. She would have to be careful. If Dilsey or the soldier saw her standing, the dancing would end, as the old saying went.

When she reached the end of the bed, she tore off the plastic cap from the top of a leg, moistened her finger, and pulled up an object that had been suspended in the hollow of the leg by a slender thread of bed linen. The object glinted in the light: a surgeon's scalpel, an instrument so sharp the mere weight of it would lacerate skin.

She held it by its thread and spun it, watching the sunlight flash on its blade. She'd stolen it from a careless doctor during one of the endless examinations. "Cough! Cough louder!" he'd said as she pulled it from the instrument tray. Then he'd touched her breast in a most undoctorlike way, and it had taken all her self-control to keep from plunging it into his heart right then and there. But instead she gritted her teeth and slid the knife discreetly under her pillow.

This would be the tool of her vengeance, she thought, watching the scalpel spin. With it she would set into motion events that would free her from this confinement and bring about the death of Nick Carter, a consummation she wanted more than anything else in the world. *Soon,* she told herself. *The time is almost at hand.*

The Americans had already parried. This she knew. How she knew was a combination of intuition and tradecraft, although which predominated was impossible to say. Her father had taught her the tricks of the agent's art—the suspicious turn of mind, the secretiveness, the prodigious powers of deduction, the constant alertness and attention to detail—at such a young age and engrained them in her so thoroughly, tradecraft and intuition had become indistinguishable in her thinking.

Three weeks ago she'd fallen asleep reading in bed and two hours had passed of which she was completely unaware. This was highly unusual. She'd always been a light sleeper, given to restless dreams, some of them so vivid they'd caused her mother a great deal of concern when Tatiana was a child.

But this was a dreamless sleep, and when she'd awakened she tasted something bitter on her lips, and her skin was achingly dry except beneath one earlobe. There was wax. Conclusion? Her food had been drugged, and while she was unconscious a wax impression had been made of her face. There could be only one reason: they were making a double of her to fool her father.

Whether or not this operation had succeeded, she had no idea. Daily she searched the faces of everyone around her for some clue, but their expressions revealed nothing. They were too stupid to be told, she concluded. And yet she lost sleep each night wondering if she'd unwittingly become the instrument of her father's destruction.

The time is coming soon, she thought as the scalpel slowed. Soon she would be strong enough, and already the agony of not knowing was driving her into frenzies at night. Soon her own restlessness would force her to break out at any cost.

The door lock clicked, and the sound pierced Tatiana's body, bringing it rigid and alert. She was standing! For the sake of Lenin! They mustn't see her!

She hobbled to the head of the bed and tried to climb in, holding on to the bed table for support. But the table's casters shot out underneath, and it crashed to the floor—reading lamp, cards, water pitcher, everything. She scrambled under the covers just as the door flew open.

"What's going on in here?" asked Lieutenant Dilsey, staring down at the overturned table.

"I pushed it," Tatiana answered. "I was lonely. I don't like being ignored."

Dilsey's eyes went from Tatiana to the table, a dim suspicion beginning to dawn in them.

Tatiana looked down and to her horror noticed she'd left the cap off the bedpost. She still had the scalpel in her hand underneath the covers.

Dilsey picked up the table with some difficulty, then she rolled it back and forth across a small patch of floor, testing it. "These things don't fall over all that easy," she said thoughtfully. "You must have given it quite a shove."

"I was angry," said Tatiana sullenly. "I am still angry."

"You know something, Little Miss High and Mighty," said Dilsey coming closer and leaning down to the girl's face, "Bernie Green swore up and down you could walk, and I told her I thought she was crazy. 'Bernie,' I said, 'you've just let that girl get to you. She can't walk.' But you know, I'm beginning to wonder if maybe Bernie wasn't right."

Tatiana's fear at having been startled now turned into anger. This, coupled with the resentment she'd harbored for weeks against this woman and the one they called Green, quickly proved too much for her restraint. With a lightning motion, she pulled out her hand with the scalpel set firmly in her fist and slashed the old woman's face, splitting the eyebrow, the eye, the nose, and opening a long slash in the cheek.

So quick was this movement and so fluid—and the scalpel so sharp—that Dilsey was not even fully aware of what had happened. She pulled back with a look of amazement, holding her hands out in front of her and examining the blood that was now rushing in a torrent from her face, down her neck, and dripping onto the floor. Slowly, as she realized what she was looking at, her mouth parted and she screamed a soundless scream.

In a flash Tatiana threw back the covers and jumped out of bed. She was still weak, but she managed to get behind the terrified Dilsey and loop an arm around her throat. "Not a sound, you silly bitch!" she hissed in the nurse's ear, holding the scalpel against the old woman's jugular. "One scream and I'll cut your head off!"

Dilsey was still looking at the blood dripping from her hands. She tasted its saltiness in her mouth. A whimper started deep in her throat, and her hands began to shake.

"Stop whining like a dog!" whispered Tatiana. Her legs were tiring. She was going to have to do this quickly. "Call the sergeant! Call him!"

"Sergeant," Dilsey said, her voice more a plea than a command. The door didn't open. "Sergeant!" she shouted in desperation.

The door unlocked and the sergeant came in. His eyes widened when he saw the nurse. "Holy . . . what the . . ." he stammered.

"Throw down your rifle or I'll kill her!" Tatiana said.

The sergeant's rifle clattered to the floor.

"Now—slowly—hand me your service revolver."

He undid the flap of his holster and held the gun out butt first, his eyes riveted on Tatiana.

Tatiana shoved the old woman toward the door until she was close enough to grab the gun. Dilsey offered little resistance. Once she had it, Tatiana quickly changed hands, flinging the scalpel across the room and putting the gun to Dilsey's head.

"If you don't do exactly as I say, I am going to kill this silly woman, is that clear?" asked Tatiana evenly.

The sergeant nodded, backing up to let the two women out the door.

"I'm going to the Soviet embassy in Washington. I need a car and a driver. Run. Tell your superiors what has happened. Tell them to have a car waiting at the front door to the hospital. Tell them if they don't, they will scrape this woman's insides from the corridor wall. Run, pig, run!"

The sergeant hesitated only a split second, then turned, ran up the hall, and disappeared through a set of double doors.

"Now tell me the way out of here, bitch," she hissed, turning to the old woman. "And no tricks. If you try to trick me, I'll kill you."

She pushed Dilsey forward, still holding her by the neck, the gun barrel pressed against the back of her head. As they shuffled along, Tatiana half pushed and half leaned on Dilsey for support. It was only Dilsey's momentary confusion and pain that prevented her from realizing she was practically carrying the younger woman out of the hospital.

Word spread quickly, and along the corridors nurses, doctors, patients, and MP's stopped to stare at them as they passed, the number of onlookers steadily increasing until they reached the front lobby, which was filled with military police, guns drawn.

A young black man in a green uniform crisscrossed with white patent leather belts and a sergeant's patch on his arm called for them to halt.

"You cannot bluff me!" shouted Tatiana. "You will not endanger one of your own, even if she is old and of use to no one. Stand back!"

The sergeant looked around helplessly. An officer standing in a corner gave a slight nod, and the sergeant gestured for his men to clear a path.

"Do not think I will not shoot her or that if I am shot from behind I will not have time to squeeze the trigger before I fall. I assure you I am highly trained, and right now my life counts for nothing."

Dozens of pairs of anxious eyes watched as the two women lockstepped toward the large front doors, one in a hospital gown and one with a gaping cut across her face from which blood still ran.

They stopped short of the big glass front doors, and Tatiana shouted to a nearby soldier to open them. He cast an uncertain glance at his sergeant, who nodded reluctantly, then he went out and held a door open for them.

A dirty, green, late-model sedan with INTERAGENCY MOTOR POOL painted on the side idled at the curb. It was thirty yards away down two flights of cement steps, but it looked like a million steps and an equal number of miles away. Tatiana's legs were like rubber bands stretched way beyond the snapping point. More and more she counted on the nurse to hold her up.

As they made their way slowly down the stairs, the thought of finally sitting down in the car began to gain importance in Tatiana's mind. It loomed larger and larger, blotting out everything else, until she no longer cared whether she got to the embassy or stopped Nick Carter from killing her father. Just to sit and rest her legs seemed the most important thing in the world.

And yet she sensed there was something wrong with the car. Intuition told her all this had been too easy. Surely they must have tampered with the automobile. She had no proof. Everything looked all right. But her instincts said no, and her father had taught her to trust her instincts.

"Get rid of that car!" she shouted to the men around her. "Bring me another. A cab. A city cab from Washington." She remembered how long the ride from downtown Washington had taken. She had counted the minutes, even though she'd been blindfolded. She would give them just that long and no longer, leaving them no time to tamper with the vehicle.

The lieutenant conferred at the bottom of the stairs with the sergeant and two plainclothesmen.

"Get rid of it now, or I'll drop her where she stands."

"All right, all right," said the lieutenant, motioning for her to calm down. "It'll take a few minutes."

"I know exactly how long it will take! Be quick about it."

In a few seconds the sedan jumped forward with a bark of its tires and was gone, leaving Tatiana and Dilsey alone on the sidewalk, encircled by a cadre of military police.

Minutes passed. The figures of the men began to swim in front of her eyes, causing Tatiana to grip the gun tighter and press it more firmly into Dilsey's scalp. Dilsey gradually regained some of her composure and began to talk to the girl.

"I need help," she said. "This cut has to be stitched. If it isn't closed soon, I'll lose too much blood. I'll pass out."

"Stop crying, old woman. If I can stand, you can stand. Remember, if you go down, I go down with you, and you'll get the first bullet."

Tatiana's legs felt like overcooked strands of spaghetti, and she tasted sweat at the corner of her mouth in spite of the balmy October breeze.

Ten minutes. Fifteen minutes. The lieutenant pulled back his coat sleeve and checked his watch. Hadn't he just done that a few seconds ago? And weren't they drawing closer, all of them? Did they sense she was on the verge of letting go completely, falling down, not caring any longer what happened to her, just to be able to ease the pain in her legs for a few minutes?

A cab jerked to a halt in front of the hospital, a big yellow Plymouth with CAPITAL CAB and a logo on the door. With the last of her strength she pushed Dilsey toward its passenger side, but Dilsey balked.

"I'm not getting in there. I'll never get out," she said with finality.

Tatiana put her mouth close to Dilsey's ear. Her only hope lay in frightening the old woman into submission. "Dilsey!" she whispered. "This is the voice of your death, woman. Listen! You are nothing to me. Less than nothing. You have pained me. And for weeks I swore I would kill you when I got the chance. I killed my first man when I was twelve, a soldier who tried to rape me. Since then I've killed others. Many others. If it weren't for more pressing matters, I would kill you now just for the pleasure of watching you die. And let them hang me! Do you understand? Take my advice, you dried-up old bitch, and don't tempt me."

The old woman's head shook with terror and her eyes stared dumbly forward.

"Now, move!" Tatiana pushed her haltingly toward the car. "The door! Open it!" The passenger door swung open and scraped against the sidewalk. Then, still gripping the old nurse tightly, Tatiana sat down and pulled Dilsey in with her. "Drive!" she ordered. The driver hit the accelerator, and the door slammed shut with the momentum.

As they sped toward the camp's front gate, she transferred the gun to the driver, lodging it firmly against his temple. "The Soviet embassy and stop for nothing. Nothing, do you understand?"

"Anything you say, lady."

They shot through the gate and out onto the open road. A column of motorcycle-riding military police fell into line behind them, sirens blaring and lights flashing. They followed at a discreet distance until the cab turned north on the highway, then a few of them passed so there were motorcycles fore and aft.

The speedometer needle rose to sixty and stayed there. The driver was a big black man, and behind his thick beard his face revealed a grim determination not to be afraid. As he drove, Tatiana kept the big revolver close against his head.

"Think you could point that thing the other way, lady?" he asked finally. "It's a little hard to drive with that thing in my face like that."

Without saying a word, Tatiana pulled the hammer back until it clicked into a cocked position.

"I get the picture," he said.

Dilsey stared with empty eyes out the window. The life seemed to have drained out of her.

The cab swung onto the on-ramp of the highway. The two lead motorcycles' flashing taillights turned to solid red as brakes were applied.

"They want us to slow down," said the driver.

"No slowing!" shouted Tatiana nervously.

"I got to, lady. They're holding me back."

Tatiana hit the horn in a long blast that made Dilsey jump. The big Harleys shot forward, widening the gap between them and the cab.

"Keep moving!"

As they pulled onto the highway, the nation's capital became visible in the distance. "Almost there," said the driver.

The radio spit. "Tatiana," said a voice. "Tatiana Kobelev, can you hear me?"

In her highly excited state, Tatiana flinched at the sound of her name. She grabbed the cabby's shoulder, digging the gun even more firmly into the side of his head.

"Easy, lady," he said. "It's just the radio. Somebody wants to talk."

Her eyes wildly searched the dashboard until she saw the microphone. She picked it up with her free hand and keyed the microphone. "This is Tatiana Kobelev. Who is this?"

"Special Agent Parks. FBI. We've been in contact with the Soviet embassy, and they say you are not welcome. Repeat, not welcome. We have the chargé d'affaires on his way here to talk to you now."

"Turn it off," Tatiana told the driver. He reached over and flipped the switch, and they rode the rest of the way downtown in silence.

In a large office on Pennsylvania Avenue, across the city from the speeding taxicab, Undersecretary of State Paul Lathrop was reading a file spread out on his desk. John Mills, National Security Advisor to President Manning, watched attentively from an easy chair a few feet away, his expression haggard, his fingers nervously twisting a ballpoint pen. Standing behind him, hands in pockets, David Hawk stared out the window at the east face of the White House, which was just up the street, a cigar clenched tightly in his teeth.

Undersecretary Lathrop finished his reading, closed the

file jacket, and cleared his throat, breaking a silence that had lasted several minutes.

"Gentlemen," he said, "am I being led to believe that Millicent Stone—who attempted an assassination of President Manning and who eventually committed suicide by hanging herself in her cell and whose diary we have all read in the national media—did not in fact pull the trigger?"

"That's right, Paul. A hoax," said Mills, squinting his eyes and fluttering his lashes as though the truth spoken aloud caused him no small measure of physical pain.

"And that the real assassin, some Russian girl who's been illegally detained in a base hospital somewhere. . ."

"Camp Peary."

"Yes, Camp Peary, has kidnapped a cab driver and a nurse and right now is on her way to the Soviet embassy here in Washington to seek asylum?"

"That's the long and short of it, yes."

"I'm finding all this rather difficult to believe. The thought that the American government would deliberately suppress information of such a grave nature—"

"Spare us the speech, Paul. The girl will be at the embassy door in a few minutes. Just sign the order."

"I'm afraid my conscience won't allow me to let a woman like this off scot-free."

"We don't have much choice. If the Secretary himself were here, I'd have him order you to sign, but Bill's out of the country, so I'm asking you as a friend. Sign it and do it quickly."

"I still don't know why you come to me. Why don't you sign it? Or better yet, let Manning handle it."

"It'll look more attractive this way, on down the line, if it comes from the lowest possible level."

"They don't want to get their hands dirty," Hawk growled, turning around. "Nobody wants the responsibility."

"Then I'm not sure I do either," said Lathrop, pushing the file onto Mills's side of the desk.

"Listen to me," said Mills, rising. "We can't detain her, because legally she doesn't exist. And now that she's out in the open, she's becoming an embarrassment. I talked to the President not twenty minutes ago, and the decision has been made. We're going to just let her go with as little stink as possible, even if the Russians don't want her, which I have just been informed they don't. Now dammit, Paul, if the President can forgive and forget, why can't you? After all, he was the one she was shooting at."

Lathrop stared belligerently up at Mills. "I don't take kindly to being coerced."

Mills sank back into his chair with a sigh. Then he took off his glasses and made a production of cleaning them. "Let me put it this way," he said, examining the lenses carefully. "The President would consider it a great personal favor if you would sign."

Lathrop looked down pensively at the typewritten sheet sticking out from the bottom cover of the file jacket. "The President told you to tell me that?"

"He did."

Then it was Lathrop's turn to sigh. "Where's a pen?"

Mills quickly handed him the one in his hand. As Lathrop scratched his signature, Hawk tapped Mills's shoulder and drew him across the room.

"I have to be going," he said.

"I understand. Thanks for coming. Your being here added a lot of necessary weight."

"You know this isn't how I wanted the Kobelev woman handled," Hawk said.

Mills nodded. "The President tells me we have an agent in Europe who may be seriously compromised if the girl is loose. But you have to understand our position, too. For the safety of the nation, we covered up a rather serious crime. Someday it will all come out in the wash, but can you imagine what would happen right now if the American public were to find out the KGB itself ran an operation in this country to kill the President? With tensions between our two countries on the rise of late? This agent of ours, he's a pretty good man?"

"The best. He's also a personal friend."

"He'll be all right, you think?"

Hawk shook his head doubtfully. "He's gotten himself out of some rough scrapes before, but this time he's up against some pretty stiff competition. We'll just have to wait and see."

NINE

Carter's heavy Luger thudded to the floor of the salon car, and was quickly scooped up by one of Kobelev's guards and placed on the bar. He squeezed through the small vent, hung for a moment, then dropped to his feet. The guard immediately grabbed his shoulder and shoved him into a swivel chair. Then the second guard, who had waylaid Carter on the roof, dropped into the car and took up a position by the back door.

Kobelev set his vodka glass on the bar and picked up the Luger. He ejected the clip from the butt, then turned and fired into the wall, the bullet in the firing chamber making a *chunk* sound as it splintered the paneling.

"You *did* mean business," he said.

Cynthia sat in front of the bar, her head slumped forward, seemingly unconscious. She was held into her wheelchair with sashes of bedsheet.

"Really, Carter, I'm rather disappointed. You've taken all this entirely too personally," he went on.

"What have you done to Cynthia?" Carter asked harshly.

"Cynthia?" Kobelev looked over, eyebrows arched, as though he'd forgotten completely she was there. "Is that her name? We hadn't time to administer the usual injections to get any information out of her."

"What did you do to her?"

"No reason to become alarmed, dear boy. She's simply

asleep. We find she's a bit easier to handle this way. No need to worry, though. Gregor here is an expert at such things. Isn't that right, Gregor?"

The guard by the door smiled broadly. His hair had been shaved into a brown stubble, as was that of the guard who watched attentively by the bar.

"Do you like my little family?" asked Kobelev. "I found them in a monastery in the Urals. Their order has been fighting Cossacks for centuries. Natural-born assassins, each of them."

"Including. . ."

"Including Shurin? Yes." Kobelev suddenly switched on what looked to be a shortwave radio that rested on the bar. Immediately sounds of struggle emanated from the speaker, grunts of effort and loud scraping noises, then silence and the voice of the assistant chef: "*Mon Dieu, monsieur!* We did not think you would live!" Kobelev switched it off. "I always wire each of my men. It allows me to be in many places at the same time. Show him, Gregor."

The guard pulled up his thick turtleneck sweater to reveal a tiny microphone taped to his brawny chest.

"I am a difficult man to surprise."

"I see that," said Carter.

"But there is no reason to steal in here like a thief, Mr. Carter," Kobelev continued, taking his drink and sitting himself across the low cocktail table from Carter. "I've been looking forward to seeing you again. As I said before, you're taking this business entirely too personally. I do my job, you do yours, but there is no reason we can't remain friends. We are alike, you and I, men of action, inclined to be a little ruthless when it comes to something we want."

"You're crazy. Sending your own daughter to kill the President of the United States. What on earth did you hope to accomplish besides World War III?"

"Power, to put it simply. One has to think boldly, act boldly. Have you read Napoleon's memoirs?"

"No."

"You should. He has a wealth of advice for men like us. But you mentioned my daughter."

"We still have her," said Carter, brightening.

"Yes. She's well, I trust?"

"Afraid not. Had to put a bullet in her to keep her from killing the President. Lodged against her spine. Doctors say she'll never walk again."

Kobelev stared darkly into the bottom of his vodka. "That's bitter news," he said. "Bitter news, indeed. I hate the sight of a cripple. I truly do." He abruptly threw down the rest of the clear liquid and set the glass with a sharp *clack* on the tabletop. "Is that why the wheelchair for the decoy?" he asked.

"We thought it lent a touch of authenticity. We couldn't be sure how much you knew."

"I see. I want her back, Carter. Immediately! If Tatiana is not returned to me, I shall have to torture our little decoy here until she tells me where my daughter is being kept and I will mount a rescue operation of my own."

"What if I told you Cynthia doesn't know where Tatiana is?"

"That would be most unfortunate. Most likely, then, she will not survive the interrogation." Kobelev took up his glass and headed back to the bar. "There will have to be some sort of time limit, of course," he said. "Shall we say, then, that Tatiana must be returned here to me before the train reaches Istanbul, or I cannot be responsible for this young lady's safety?"

The eyes of each of the guards followed Kobelev as he went behind the bar to get the vodka bottle. Carter reached up and yanked the emergency-brake cord that ran through grommets just over the window. There was an ear-piercing screech of metal. Everything pitched forward. Kobelev smashed headlong into the liquor cabinet behind the bar, and the two guards sprawled on the floor. Cynthia, her wheelchair unlocked, rolled against the bar, tipped forward, then came down hard, her head lolling back and forth from the impact.

Carter snatched up his Luger and charged the door. He pulled it open just as a bullet whined off the metal jamb inches from his head. Another shot was fired as he ducked into the passageway between cars.

Two windows took the place of the double Dutch doors he'd found behind the dining car, and although the frames were old, the glass looked new, double plated and heavily insulated. He pulled up one frantically, but it was bolted shut. For a fleeting instant, he considered smashing it, but the thought of jumping through a hole surrounded by jagged pieces of glass held no appeal for him, and he threw open the door into the next car instead.

Everything in here was pandemonium. Most of the passengers had been catapulted from their seats. Several held their heads, and there seemed to be a great deal of blood.

Carter glanced quickly around, trying to find the guard he'd been told was stationed here. A knot of people stood over a figure stretched out in the middle of the aisle. Through the crowd he caught a glimpse of the telltale blue turtleneck and the shaved head. Apparently the guard had been the only one standing when the brakes locked.

Without waiting to find out if the man was seriously injured, Carter mounted the backs of two seats, pushed off the lid of the vent hole, and was in the process of wriggling his way out when someone yelled "Halt!" in Russian. A shot sounded and something solid hit the edge of his shoe.

He pulled out of the hole just as another bullet creased his trouser leg, then he scrambled to his feet, took two quick steps and was over the side, falling for what seemed an eternity. He landed hard, fell forward, and tumbled.

Shouts in German pierced the air. It wasn't the guards. He raised his head a few inches over the top of the weeds. Two flashlight beams moved jerkily down the train, stopping now and then and darting in among the wheels.

It was the brakeman and the Russian engineer. There was nothing wrong with the train, the brakeman said, but he'd heard gunshots. In very bad German the engineer told him they were none of his business.

The two examined the entire length of the train, then came hurriedly up the other side. After a pause the whistle blew, indicating the steam was up, and the big pushrods put the giant steel wheels into motion. A short time later Carter stood alone on the tracks, and the air held nothing but the night wind and the distant pounding of the train as it gathered speed away from him.

Rodya Alexandrovitch Zemin, a stoop-shouldered, paunchy man in a well-cut, custom-tailored suit, handed Tatiana a glass of water, then watched grimly as she drank. He clasped his hands behind his back, a posture that drew apart the panels of his jacket, making his large stomach all the more noticeable.

She studied him over the rim of her glass. He had changed, she mused. The man had helped forge the new KGB from the old Cheka. By sheer force of his will and determination he had risen, along with her father, to the top echelons of power. He had been a veritable living legend at Moscow Center. But now? Hair fashionably styled and blow-dried, sleek like the polished surface of an American automobile. Heavy jowls giving him a prosperous look, complementing his huge middle bulging with good food and fine wines. Well-oiled and fat, she decided, like one of Caesar's generals. In America wealth corrupted everything.

"Feeling better?" he asked, taking the empty glass and placing it on the desk.

"Some, thank you, Comrade. I am tired and weak, but I still have a long way to go."

"I imagine you are most eager to return to the homeland and see your father."

"Yes, I am. I have failed in my mission, but I am sure he will still want to see me."

"Yes," said Zemin, and a nervous silence followed during which he gazed at the floor, still working his hands together behind his back. Finally he pulled a chair across the bare parquet floor and sat down facing her. "Comrade Kobelev, may I speak freely?"

"Address me as Tanya, please. It reminds me of the old days when you tossed me on your knee at my father's *dacha*."

"Tanya," he began, his hands now resting on the desk in front of him, looking like two pink starfish, "things have changed at home since you have been gone. Your father has, how shall I say it, fallen from grace. They have confiscated his *dacha* and his Moscow apartment. There have been unfavorable articles in *Pravda*. Directives have been issued restricting his security clearance. His position, I am afraid, is in grave jeopardy. Even Nerchinsky, his most avid supporter on the Presidium, has been questioned, particularly in regard to this last operation in the United States. Charges may be forthcoming."

"Is this why I was told I was not welcome here in the embassy of my own country?"

"We had to make a quick decision, Tanya. Of course we did not realize how much the Americans themselves wanted to be rid of you. But you must understand our position: turmoil at home over what you and your father have done; our negotiations with the West in a shambles; official Washington turning a very cold shoulder to us. There was a time a few weeks ago when I greatly feared we'd be expelled!"

"You put too much stock in relations with these Western hedonists," Tatiana said sullenly. "They are unimportant. Coexistence itself is unimportant. That is the message my father brings to all the Russian people."

"Perhaps, my dear," said Zemin with a sigh, "but perhaps, too, the Presidium has decided to take a more liberal course."

"Perhaps again," said Tatiana, "but it may also be another ploy of my father's to consolidate his power. It would not be the first time he's acted in secret and in such a way as to keep the entire world, even Moscow Center, guessing. Where is my father now?"

"Aboard a train. The Orient Express. The Americans very much want to see your father dead, it seems. They engineered a trap using an actress impersonating you. He rose to it, took the actress and an entire trainload of people, and is now demanding your release. I might add we would know nothing of this if it weren't for the diligence of the train's engineer who realized your father was acting without Moscow's consent and phoned our contact in Rheims."

"My father is a daring man, is he not? An entire train at gunpoint, across Europe. Imagine! And no less prestigious a train than the Orient Express! All those bourgeois Europeans in their tuxedos and evening gowns! What greater proof of a father's love could a daughter ask for? I must see him! I must!"

"That may be difficult to arrange, Tatiana Nikolaiyevna, although I understand he is keeping the train's original schedule. At least he has some sense of the embarrassment he is causing us, one and all."

"But I must see him! You must arrange it, Comrade."

Zemin's plump features compressed in an unpleasant way.

"But you must! We are old friends, let us not forget that. Surely my father would do as much or more . . ."

Zemin sighed heavily and looked hard at the young woman in front of him. "I will see what I can do," he said at last. "The Americans seem willing to let you go, and the dust at home has not yet cleared. I am not sure where your father stands . . ." He would have finished, but in her excitement Tatiana had already leaped from her chair and was squeezing him in an affectionate bear hug that made talking difficult.

"Easy, dear child, easy," he said with an indulgent smile, extricating himself from her embrace. "It may very well be I'm cutting my throat by helping you."

"Yes, Rodya Alexandrovitch, I understand. But thank you! Thank you!"

"So," he said, standing, "I will arrange your transportation. But you must leave immediately. I fear any minute a directive will come forbidding me to extend aid in any way." He went behind the desk and picked up the phone. Tatiana watched him dial, but then a thought occurred to her.

"Did they mention if an agent named Nick Carter happened to be involved in any attempt to kill my father?"

Zemin shook his head. "I don't remember the name. Hello?" he said into the phone. "Gregoriev? Do you still have that contact in Havana? Good. I have a job for you . . ."

Tatiana sat back into her chair, considering. If there'd been a plot to kill her father, it was possible Nick Carter was in on it, she thought pleasantly. And if it had gone awry, he couldn't be too far away. No further, say, than the range of a pistol shot. She smiled at the prospect.

It seemed to Carter that he'd been walking for hours. The grassy embankment below the railroad track had given out onto a vast marshy plain covered by a ground fog, which at times extended no higher than his knees and at other times churned around him in the wake of a gust of wind, obscuring his vision altogether. Occasionally, when the fog cleared, he saw the moon dance on a body of water in the distance, and although it was difficult to make out, he guessed it to be rather large. No lights were visible on the opposite shore. There had been lights earlier, however, much closer, and although they'd gone out more than an hour ago, he still walked in that direction, hoping to find some sign of habitation.

He pulled the collar of his chef's jacket up around his ears and fastened the top button of the lapel under his chin. The groundwater was only a few inches deep, but it had soaked his pants to the thighs, and now the wind whipped the wet cloth against his skin, chilling him thoroughly.

As he walked he stuffed his hands in his pockets to keep them warm, and after a few dozen steps he had to wade through a pile of wet weeds. They looked to be the refuse of some sort of dredging operation. They formed a small mound seven or eight feet high. He climbed the mound until he balanced precariously on a perch that afforded him a view of the entire area.

Dead ahead no more than two hundred yards, outlined in dark gray against an even darker background, stood a shack on a cluster of pilings. A pier ran off to the north from which a rickety ladder extended to the water's surface. Next to the ladder a small shallow-draft boat bobbed like a cork.

He hurried down the other side and splashed toward it. The water deepened quickly, and by the time he reached the ladder, it was up to his waist. He climbed until his eyes were level with the weatherbeaten pier, then he stopped, taking in every aspect. Everything seemed quiet. Except for the steady drip of water from his wet clothes and the soft sucking of the waves in the pilings, the night was quiet. An eider duck cooed to its mate in the distance. This place seemed deserted, and yet he was sure this was where he'd seen lights earlier.

He hurried across to the shack and listened at the door. The unmistakable drone of snoring came from within. Back at the pier, he looked down at the little open boat, bobbing in the moonlight.

She looked seaworthy, but there was no way to propel her. He looked around and for the first time noticed two sets of oars attached to the shack's outer wall. He went over and was lifting one down when something scattered over the boards by his feet caught his eye.

He stooped down, picked up some, and rubbed it between his fingers. Sawdust. But what on earth would someone be sawing out here? Then it dawned on him. It had nothing to do with carpentry. It was packing material, the kind used to fill the spaces between bottles and other delicate things during shipment.

Then he looked across to where the moon made stepping-stones on the water. The Neusiedlersee! He should have realized. Austria on one shore, Hungary on the other, and in the middle a hot little traffic in Western goods.

He pulled out his Luger, went around to the front, and boldly kicked in the door. A balding little man sat bolt upright in his makeshift bed on the floor, his eyes wide as saucers. "*Wer ist da?*" he stammered.

"*Amerikaner,*" Carter answered, making sure the Luger in his hand was clearly visible in the shaft of moonlight from the open door.

The eyes narrowed. "*Polizei?*"

"*Nein.*"

"Then what is it?" he demanded, indicating the gun.

"The next time you and your friends make a run, there'll be an additional piece of contraband floating across the lake."

"*Ja?*"

"Me."

• • •

Over the course of the next two hours Carter learned a great deal about the man in the shack and his dabbling in illegal exports. His name, he said, was Friedrich Schwetzler, although he'd been christened Ferenc Balassa. He was a Hungarian who'd fled during the uprisings of 1956. He'd crossed the border here by boat, planning to go west to France, or maybe even to the United States, but unforeseen circumstances forced him to leave his wife and small daughter behind, and he hadn't the heart to go any further than eastern Austria. So here he'd stayed, gotten a job as a waiter in the hotel in Bruck, and begun smuggling. His wife had since died, and his daughter now had children of her own. The smuggling allowed him to keep in contact with her and her family. His agent on the other side was his son-in-law.

They smuggled in more than just cases of wine and sought-after Western clothes, he told Carter. There were political items as well; Western newspapers, forbidden manuscripts, even parts of Solzhenitsyn's works had passed through his hands.

As they talked, the fog outside lifted, but Schwetzler said that the moonlight made it too dangerous to attempt a crossing tonight, and his son-in-law would not come. Tomorrow night would be safer. Carter was crestfallen. In his mind's eye the Orient Express steamed off into the night, putting another mile between them for every minute he delayed.

That night he slept on the floor of Schwetzler's tiny apartment in downtown Bruck, and in the morning stood with a line of tourists outside the telephone exchange, waiting to make an overseas call.

He felt much better than he had the night before, even though he'd slept only fitfully. The day had dawned bright and clear, and the weather forecast called for falling temperatures and fog by evening, which meant the son-in-law would definitely appear. He had at last shed his chef's uniform, which after his fighting and tramping through several miles of swamp had become little more than rags, and had donned instead some clothes Schwetzler had lent him: thick corduroy pants, a black wool sweater, and a peasant's cap that gave him a roguish, rural look. So now as the streets began to fill, and workers brushed by him on their way to work, and women in black babushkas and overcoats began to appear, pushing their carts to market, Carter blended right in and began to feel, to his own amazement, that he actually belonged here.

The telephone exchange opened at the stroke of eight, and Carter filed in with the crowd, gave the operator the safe number in Washington, then retired to a corner to wait for his connection to be made. In his borrowed clothes no one paid him any mind, and within a few minutes he was in a booth listening to the impatient voice of David Hawk.

"Our ruse with Cynthia didn't last two minutes with Kobelev. He knew immediately she wasn't his daughter, and now he wants Tatiana back or he's going to kill Cynthia. We need some sort of safe house somewhere along the train route in case we have to make an exchange. And I need Tatiana on this side of the Atlantic. I may have to dangle her under his nose a bit to get Cynthia away from him."

"It's not going to be that easy, Nick," Hawk grumbled.

Carter held his silence. He had a bad feeling.

"We don't have the girl. She escaped. This afternoon."

"She had help?"

"No. She evidently isn't crippled." Hawk quickly explained what had happened, at the hospital and then later.

"Why wasn't she stopped, sir?" Carter asked. This entire thing was starting to go very bad.

Hawk sighed deeply. "Wasn't much we could do about it, really. We covered up the fact she was the one who tried to kill the President. We held her in the hospital. We could hardly let that out now." Hawk was silent for a moment. "There were a lot of reputations on the line. We didn't want another Watergate, with the press all over us and the President. It would have been disastrous. I don't think they wanted her over at her own embassy either. But they took her." Again there was the silence. "In the end she was a defecting spy who'd had a change of heart. No waves."

"Makes things a bit difficult here."

"There was nothing to be done about it, Nick. Nothing."

"Is she still at her embassy?"

"We don't think so. Manville thinks she shipped out in disguise. Probably on the plane to Cuba. From there . . . ?"

"Yes, sir," Carter said. "That means she'll be on her way here."

"I'm assigning you some help. Lieutenant Commander j.g. Stewart. Naval Intelligence."

"Never heard the name."

"Mediterranean fleet. East European Theater expert."

"What's the contact routine?"

"It's all taken care of, Nick. You have the passive role. You know when the time comes. Meanwhile, good luck."

"Thanks," Carter said. He hung up, paid the operator at the desk, and stepped outside. Somehow the sunlight didn't seem nearly as bright and hopeful as it had ten minutes before.

TEN

Carter spent the remainder of the morning at the sidewalk café attached to the hotel. It was virtually deserted in October, most of the tourists having either gone home or moved on to the Alps to await the snow for skiing; and although it was cool in the shade, Carter managed to stay warm by sipping hot coffee and eating apple strudel while he pored over the Parisian papers.

At noon the whistle blew in the shoe factory down the street, and in a few minutes the café was inundated with sallow-faced secretaries and pimply mail clerks eager to enjoy the favorable turn in the weather. They talked amiably and joked until one o'clock, when they all disappeared as suddenly as they'd come, leaving Carter alone to drink his sixth or seventh coffee and to peruse a week-old edition of *The New York Times* the waiter had found for him in the lobby. He was leafing through the front section when he chanced to look up and notice that not all the young people had left. An attractive girl in skin-tight designer jeans and an American ski parka sat three or four tables away, staring at him. He quickly turned back to his reading, but not before he'd taken account of the lovely auburn tint in her hair, her wide, sea green eyes, and most particularly, her tanned skin.

He'd read another half dozen paragraphs, not really digesting any of it, when he heard her chair scrape against the pavement. Looking up, he saw her standing over him, the parka hanging open, revealing a beautifully suggestive curve beneath her buttoned-up sweater. She had prostitute written all over her.

"Mind if I sit down?" she asked in a street German.

"*Macht nichts,*" he shrugged. He turned a page and studied the headlines. He looked up shortly and found her staring at him again.

"I'm wondering what kind of man you are."

"A busy one. Too busy for fun and games, I'm afraid. Maybe some other time."

"What do you think I am?" she protested indignantly but with a shade of astonishment, as though what he were implying were so out of line it wasn't to be believed.

"I don't think you want me to tell you. Let me just say I haven't any money for your services today."

Her mouth fell open in surprise, then a cloud of anger rolled in behind the sea green eyes. "Schweinhund . . ." she started to say, but he was ahead of her, having already stood and folded the paper under his arm.

"That's not to say you're not pretty," he went on, "or that I might not enjoy it another time, but not today."

If this were an attempt to smooth things over, it failed miserably. A mixture of surprise and anger continued to mount in the girl's face until it seemed as if she'd lost the ability to talk. "W-What? W-What 'it'?" she stuttered.

Carter didn't bother to reply. He turned his back to her, crossed the café, paid his bill at the bar, then left the hotel by the front door.

He went straight to Schwetzler's apartment. Schwetzler was sitting in an armchair, gun oil, rags, and pieces of revolver laid out on the table beside him.

"Fog tonight," he said, greeting Carter cheerfully. He sighted up the barrel to see if it was clean. "That's how it is. During the day sun. Then at night the air cools and fog. A climate suitable for smugglers, yes? And the air is damp today. Should be a thick one."

Carter went to the window and pulled back the drape. Down in the street on the opposite corner the girl strained to look first in one direction, then in the other. Apparently she'd lost him when he turned in from the main street.

"Friedrich," he said, calling him over. "Know her?"

Schwetzler looked down over Carter's shoulder. "No," he said after a moment's study. "But I'd like to, even at my age. Is she an agent?"

"I don't know."

They watched as the girl shrugged and retraced her steps up the side street. "If she isn't," Carter said, "I just blew one of the better opportunities of my life."

The fog was everything Schwetzler had promised. It hung in the air like a curtain, impeding pedestrians and slowing automobile traffic to a crawl. They drove out the lake road until it became little more than a cart path, and they lost sight of it even in the high beams. Schwetzler parked, and they went the rest of the distance on foot.

The skiff was moored to a single piling in a sea of reeds that obscured it completely from view. Carter was amazed his companion was able to find it.

"We do this two, sometimes three nights a week in heavier fog than this," he explained. "Tonight is easy. Usually I have heavy boxes to carry."

They got into the boat, and Schwetzler began rowing. In the fog the night seemed to close around them with only the occasional bleat of a foghorn to the northwest to orient them.

"How do you find the shack in all this?" Carter asked.

"I hear it. The waves play a tune on the pilings. Listen!" He held up a finger for quiet. "There it is!" He turned several degrees starboard and continued to row.

Even with Schwetzler's sonar guidance, it took them half an hour to reach the shack. Once there, they waited another hour and a half before they heard the first slow *chug-chug* of a diesel engine growing steadily closer.

"*Hallo! Wer ist da?*" called a voice.

"Why is he speaking German?" Carter asked suspiciously, grabbing Schwetzler's arm.

"What would you have him speak in these waters? Hungarian? *Hier!*" Schwetzler called back.

The lumbering hull of a fishing boat appeared out of the mist and nuzzled itself against the pier. Her sole occupant, a young man in a black sweater and sailor's watch cap, threw over a line and Schwetzler secured it.

"Nicholas, this is my son-in-law, Erno Vadas," Schwetzler said as the young man stepped onto the pier.

"Erno, this is Nicholas Carter. He is . . ."

"*Ein Amerikaner,*" finished Vadas, shaking Carter's hand.

"Is it so obvious?"

"No, but every frontier guard from Bratislava to Szombathely is looking for you. They have orders to shoot to kill."

"Where did you hear this?" demanded Schwetzler.

"They are talking about it as far east as Györ."

"Kobelev," said Carter, turning to Schwetzler.

"But I don't understand. Why would he want you dead when he has still to negotiate for his daughter?"

"His daughter escaped. She's probably on her way to him right now."

"Then your position is very grave," said Schwetzler, shaking his head.

"Not as grave as the girl's he's holding captive."

"Do you think she is still alive?"

"Maybe. Kobelev isn't on the best of terms with his home base. It's possible he hasn't been told yet. Maybe he figures that now that I've had a chance to relay his demands to my superiors, I'm expendable. He's wanted me dead for a long time."

"Then I pity you, my friend. You are a hunted man. As a man who has also been hunted in his time, I know how it feels."

"This is idle talk," Vadas put in impatiently. "And it is not getting us any closer to Hungary. We must move now. The guard boats are double tonight."

The three men quickly set to work emptying the shack of its contents: cases of French wines, bolts of brightly colored cloth, boxes of perfume and other luxury items, and stacks of Western clothing, including denim jackets and blue jeans.

They stashed the contraband belowdecks, then Schwetzler gave Carter's hand a solemn, knowing shake, and stepped from the gunwale onto the pier. The diesel sputtered into life, and Schwetzler threw the mooring line onto the deck. Carter watched from the bridge as Schwetzler waved once; as the boat moved away, he was quickly swallowed by the fog.

The young captain spun the helm to port and headed for open water. "This boat isn't built for speed, so I take it you use the fog as a screen rather than trying to outrun them, is that it?" Carter shouted over the engine.

Vadas nodded, keeping his eyes riveted on the windshield. Carter stared uneasily at the seemingly impenetrable barrier of gray-white mist.

"The question is, how do you navigate in this pea soup? How do you keep from running aground?"

Vadas suddenly cut the engine and held up a finger. Across the water came the faint *bong* of a buoy bell. "They are placed wherever there is danger," Vadas said. "All of them sound slightly different. If one knows them well, they will lead one directly down the lake."

It was a good thing they were a musical family, Carter thought, or he'd have been reduced to trying to row across this lake in a skiff. He turned and went belowdecks. There he found a narrow bench and sat down, picking up an East German fishing catalogue from the map table, but he didn't read any of it. He just held it open on his lap and stared into space, wondering how Cynthia was doing and if she'd regained consciousness, and thinking perhaps it would be better if she hadn't.

The engine ceased while Vadas listened for a buoy. Carter listened along with him. Vadas started the engine again and veered starboard for several minutes, then pulled around to the left. At this rate their progress was erratic, Carter thought with some satisfaction, so even if the frontier guard was outfitted with sonar detection equipment, the old trawler would still be tough to intercept.

The gentle motion of the boat made him drowsy. He laid his head back against the bulwark and closed his eyes. Another stop, another moment of listening, then start again.

The galley and his surroundings began to move into the unconscious part of his mind, mixing with other images, when the engine stopped once more, and this time no bell sounded. Instead, the drone of another, much more powerful engine reverberated through the fog, growing steadily louder.

Carter jerked awake and hurried up to the bridge. Vadas turned from the helm as Carter rushed into the cabin. Two hundred yards and closing. Vadas cut the power, plunging the cabin into darkness except for a shaft of light streaming out of the gangway from below. Carter dashed down the stairs and pawed until he hit the switch. It was pitch black only for a second when a bright light beamed in through the porthole. The noise of the approaching engine whined to a peak, and the old trawler began to rock violently. Carter estimated the distance at twenty-five yards.

The lights disappeared quickly, then the engine noise diminished as it steamed into the distance. Carter came slowly up the stairs. "I can't believe they didn't see us," he said.

"The fog," said Vadas. "Be prepared. There'll be others."

They moved slowly ahead in complete darkness for the next quarter of an hour, then stopped again and listened. In the silence the night pulled itself around them, black and damp. The very atmosphere of the cabin had turned to fog. It had penetrated Carter's clothes, and its dampness filled his nostrils. In the distance a buoy tolled like a death knell.

"Funny," said Vadas. "I would have sworn that should have been on the starboard side, not the port." He hastily swung the wheel to starboard when it suddenly dawned on Carter that this was the direction from which the guard boat had been coming.

"Hey!" he shouted. "Maybe they changed the . . ."

He never completed the sentence. A deafening screech, like a million gulls all diving at once, tore through the cabin, and the deck pitched crazily, tossing Vadas off-balance and ramming his head into the control panel. He rolled against the bulwark, then onto the window, which broke. He hung for a moment by the window frame, black water surging up beneath him, then he slipped through and disappeared.

Carter had caught hold of the pilot's chair, and he clung to it, trying to keep from sliding down the floor and following Vadas. He hung by his hands for what seemed many minutes, although in reality it couldn't have been more than one or two, then managed to wedge a foot against the bulkhead alongside the gangway and swung over. Below him waves of black water lapped the cabin windows, gushing in the hole through which Vadas had vanished.

He crawled down the wall of the gangway, which now had become its floor, and found belowdecks to be in worse shape than the cabin. A fist of wet rock had pierced the hull, and water was steadily running in.

They'd run aground, although whether near shore or on some outcropping of rock in the middle of the lake was impossible to tell.

The boat creaked suddenly like a door being swung open on rusty hinges, and his perch in the gangway shifted another ten degrees from vertical. She was on the verge of rolling out. If he were caught in here, he'd drown.

He scurried back to the cabin and let himself down cautiously on the ladderlike structure of the window frame, being careful to step only where the crosspieces were welded to the top and bottom. Then, using the heel of his shoe, he kicked out the glass all the way to the edges.

He glanced briefly around the cabin, wondering if there were anything useful he might take. But there was no time, and at this crazy angle in the dark, rifling through the lockers would be next to impossible.

He raised his hands over his head and jumped. The cold water covered him, the logical extension of the fog. He began swimming even before he reached the surface, pulling himself forward, heedless of where he was going, until the wave the trawler made as it slid off the rocks washed over him.

Then he treaded water for what seemed an eternity, one more piece of flotsam amid a growing population of debris, until finally a chunk of hull large enough to support him floated by, and he pulled himself onto it.

Daylight found Carter huddled on his makeshift lifeboat, his knees tucked glumly under his chin. During the night the fog had lifted, and although he could now see where the boat had impaled itself—a rocky mass of land that he felt had no business being in the middle of the lake—he had drifted too far to swim to it. He sat, bobbing and shivering, sullenly staring at the waves peak and flatten on the vast, empty expanse of water.

The thought of Cynthia ran continually through his mind. She was coming to mean more to him than just a fellow agent in trouble, or even a woman he had once loved who was in danger and needed him, although either one of these would have been enough to make him brave the fires of hell to reach her. She was beginning to personify the entire debt Kobelev owed him, and the more he thought about it, the larger it seemed.

Vadas was dead. He had never surfaced after falling out of the boat. At one point during the night Carter had found what looked to be a wad of clothing floating with some boards on the water. He speared it with a piece of broken handrail and rolled it over. It was Vadas, his blank eyes staring out of white sockets, a pink gash dividing his forehead where he'd smashed it against the boat's control panel. This brought to ten the number of deaths since the operation against Kobelev had begun.

It was more than just the innocent lives that had been forfeited, or even the political ramifications of a man like Kobelev attaining power among America's enemies. It was more than the foiled assignment in Russia. His wanting Kobelev dead extended to his entire career as an agent. The man epitomized everything Carter had fought against; he negated everything Carter had risked his life time after time to preserve. If he failed again and Kobelev lived, he would tender his resignation, no matter what Hawk said. Success meant that much to him, and yet, as he sat watching the waves lap over the edges of his tiny raft, he never felt so far from accomplishing his goal.

He pulled a wood chip from the ragged corner of his little boat and absently tossed it into the water. It landed a few feet away and bobbed stubbornly. He watched it for a while, then noticed another object on the horizon, about the same apparent size as the wood chip but moving and growing steadily larger. Within a few minutes the faint roar of an outboard motor rose to accompany it.

It was an open boat with a woman in the back, steering. She was bearing directly for him. In a minute or two he recognized her as the girl from the café, whose advances he'd rebuffed the day before.

"I'll be damned . . ." he said half-aloud.

She cut the motor a few yards from him, and the boat drifted to a standstill inches from his feet. "Get in," she said brusquely in pure American English.

"What in hell . . . ?"

"Just get in. We haven't much time."

Carter swung a leg over and had no more than shifted his weight from the section of hull to the boat when she gunned the motor, spilling him into the bottom. He was up in time to see his tiny island of salvation slipping into the distance.

"Who the hell are you?" he asked.

"Name's Stewart. Roberta. Lieutenant Commander, junior grade. Naval Intelligence."

"You?"

"Right."

"I assumed you were a—"

"A man. I know. Everyone thinks that. Well, I'm not."

"No," he said a little weakly, "I guess not. But how did you know I'd be out here?"

"I followed you after that little meeting we had at the hotel café yesterday. You came to within a block of Friedrich Schwetzler's apartment, the local smuggler. His operation is something of a joke around here. The frontier guards tolerate it because they feel sorry for him, but I know one of the guardsmen, a buffoon named Franco. He told me if Schwetzler ever got ambitious, they would have to sink his boat. Then word came through about you, and they closed the border. I guess that meant Schwetzler, too. I was talking to Franco in the café last night, and he told me he was on a detail that moved one of the signal buoys out here in the shallows. When he thought of what that would do to Schwetzler, he laughed so hard he almost choked on his wine. Everyone knows how Schwetzler finds his way down the lake. At any rate, when Schwetzler's man didn't show up in the café at the usual time, I figured he'd gotten hung up out here. You with him."

"He got hung up, all right," said Carter solemnly. "Permanently."

"I know his wife. Poor Mardya."

After a moment's silence while they contemplated the widow's sorrow, it occurred to Carter that he should make some apology for the things he'd said to Roberta the day before. But the thought passed. "How do you know so much about what goes on around here?" he said instead.

"I teach English and Hungarian to the children of the Soviet diplomatic mission in Budapest . . . and play cat-and-mouse with the local KGB."

"Oh?" he said, taking interest. "I suppose they know about Tatiana Kobelev's escape."

"Tatiana the Brave?" The girl laughed. "The children are making a heroine of her. They compare her to Eliza running from the hounds."

Carter looked at her, trying to make the political and literary connection.

"Didn't you know that *Uncle Tom's Cabin* is required reading for well-bred Soviet children? Simon Legree is the prototype capitalist pig."

"That's an interesting interpretation," he said with a sigh.

"Yesterday they invented a new game," she went on. "One of them is Tatiana, and the other children play the American soldiers. They chase each other all over the schoolyard."

"So the word's out," Carter said. "But does *he* know?"

"Kobelev? Absolutely not. Word has it that Tatiana has expressly forbidden anyone to contact the train with the news she is free. Something about wanting to see the look of shock on a man's face when she finally shows up. We don't know who she intends to surprise."

"Me," said Carter. "That buys us a little time anyway. Where's the train now?"

"Sidetracked in Györ."

"Györ? It was due in Budapest."

"For some reason he had it pulled off the main line in Györ. He must have something in mind. He's invited the Hungarian circus to come in and entertain during the delay."

"Györ," Carter said. It seemed to suggest something just out of reach. Then suddenly he realized what it was. "We must get to Györ immediately."

Roberta shoved the accelerator as far forward as it would go, and the little boat skimmed across the water at a respectable speed. Within twenty minutes they had reached the Hungarian shore, picked up Stewart's car, a battered Fiat modest enough by Western standards but impossible for a schoolteacher in Hungary if it weren't for the fact that she worked for the Soviets, and were speeding down the main trunk road into Budapest by way of Györ. She drove while Carter talked.

"The entire U.S. intelligence community has been studying Kobelev ever since he started to emerge from the ranks of the KGB. His methodology, his networks, his plans—even his most intimate personal habits—are collated, analyzed, then rotated into the information pool that all services have access to." Roberta glanced at Carter. "I've made it a hobby," he said. "I've spent hours poring over the stuff. I know every flyspeck on every page. Kobelev's maternal grandmother was Hungarian. Her last known whereabouts is a state housing project in Györ."

"Wait a minute," said Roberta, tearing her eyes from the road for a brief second. "You don't really think Kobelev is going to interrupt his dash home just to pay his respects to his grandmother, do you?"

"You don't know him. He's a man given to dramatic gesture. In Russia when I was posing as a defector who wanted to join his ranks, he wanted to test my loyalty. He could have done it any number of ways—left himself exposed at some critical time, waiting to see what I would do, something subtle to trap me into thinking I could kill him and get away with it. But what does he do? He stages an elaborate fencing match in front of his entire family. You see? He's like a bullfighter working close to the horns. He thrives on danger. Besides, we know the grandmother is important to him. She all but saved him from an overbearing father. And we know he hasn't been out of the Soviet Union for almost a decade, so he can't have seen her lately."

"All right," said Roberta, her bright eyes flashing. The prospect of being in on the Kobelev kill obviously excited her. "Suppose you're right about the grandmother. What do we do then?"

"I lay the trap and spring it."

"What about me?"

"I want you at the train," Carter said. "No matter what does or does not happen, one of us must be on that train when it pulls out of here. Do you understand?"

She nodded solemnly, and he reached over and pecked her on the cheek.

ELEVEN

Translated from the Hungarian, the sign in the dirt and stone plot that passed for a courtyard read: "Béla Kun Housing Project. Erected 1968. Western Hungarian People's Housing Collective." Beyond the sign stood six concrete rectangles, seven stories high, each rectangle composed of many smaller rectangles, each smaller rectangle with an iron balcony railing across it, and from each balcony railing a line of wash flapped in the late morning sunlight. It was Sunday, the family day. People milled on the sidewalk, and promenaded up and down the street, laughing and talking with neighbors and pushing baby carriages.

Carter sat in Roberta's Fiat, parked in a line of cars directly across from Building "A," his eyes sifting the movement on all sides of him, alert for anything unusual.

The grandmother was definitely here—Judit Konya, age ninety-three, first floor center—and she had received a message earlier in the day that had set up a bucket-brigade conversation between her apartment door and the phone because she was too old to make it to the end of the hall. Carter knew this thanks to a garrulous maintenance man with an acute appreciation of fine Hungarian wine who was not averse to receiving several bottles as a present in exchange for a little information.

And yet even though remembering the grandmother's name, then finding it in a phone book of thousands of Hungarian names—all of which began to look alike after a few pages—was a small triumph in itself, the mere fact that she was here was no guarantee Kobelev was coming. The longer Carter sat, the more he began to suspect he wasn't, and that in his zeal to find a chink in Kobelev's armor, he had succeeded only in wasting more time, precious seconds that brought Cynthia closer and closer to the inevitable debriefing and execution deep in the bosom of Mother Russia.

He folded the newspaper he'd been using to cover his surveillance and got out of the car. A sick feeling in his stomach told him everything was going wrong. He put his hands in his pockets and walked resolutely to a small restaurant at the end of the block. Three old men playing *ultimo* on an upended crate stopped talking as he walked by, and he realized he was beginning to raise suspicions in the neighborhood, which only increased his uneasiness.

The owner-manager, a heavyset, round-faced man, was having an animated conversation with a young man at a back table in the otherwise empty room. He looked up as Carter walked in and gestured impatiently. Carter went to the counter to the phone. It was the fourth time this morning he'd made this call, and the ritual with the owner had abbreviated itself into a routine.

He was slipping, he told himself as his connection went through; he was getting sloppy. The whole block knew he was here, waiting for something, and that wasn't good. If he had any sense, he'd abandon this whole line of action.

"Nick?" Roberta Stewart was on the line.

"Anything yet?" he asked in Hungarian.

"The circus just got off. Isn't it funny how Kobelev thinks? He's kidnapped the entire train, won't let anybody off, yet he still feels he has to keep the passengers entertained. It's almost as if he's apologizing for the inconvenience."

"He's mad. I just hope his egomania proves his undoing," said Carter.

"Then there's nothing new on your end either?" she asked, a bit of anxiety spilling into her voice.

"Nothing."

"Listen, Nick, I've been thinking. Kobelev doesn't know me from Adam. He's got a whole slew of flower girls lined up here waiting to board. I could get one of those costumes real easy . . ."

"Absolutely not," said Carter, cutting her off.

"But Nick—"

"No, Commander. You've been outranked. I've changed my mind. You're not to make any attempt to board that train. Is that clear?"

"Yes, sir," she said after a long hesitation.

"I don't want to hear any more of that kind of talk. I'm coming to the conclusion Kobelev is still on board and has no intention . . . wait a minute."

The sleek outline of a black Soviet-made Zil limousine with diplomatic tags suddenly appeared in the restaurant's plate-glass window.

"I think I'm getting a bite. I'll get back to you." Carter hung up and strode out the door. The limousine moved slowly up the street, stopping every few buildings.

Carter walked briskly back to the Fiat. The Luger was in the glove compartment. He got it out, pulled the ammunition clip from the handle, and began stuffing it with the cartridges he had in his pocket. These shells, along with all other firearm paraphernalia, were forbidden to private citizens of Hungary and finding them early on a Sunday morning had been a tribute to Roberta's seemingly endless connections on this side of the border.

The limousine jerked to a stop in front of Building "A" just as Carter finished loading the pistol. He pushed it into the holster he still wore at the small of his back, then got out of the car and walked off rapidly in the opposite direction.

When he reached the middle of the block, he crossed over and started back down the other side. Two men had gotten out of the limo and stood with their hands thrust deep in the pockets of their trench coats. They glanced up and down the sidewalk. The usual KGB goon squad, thought Carter. A moment later a man with an unmistakable mane of snow white hair climbed out of the back seat. It was Kobelev.

At the corner Carter ducked right and raced across a soccer

field to the back of Building "B." The rear door stood ajar. He slipped in and hurried down the basement steps.

Normally, he would have set this up along the lines of the classic sniper's approach: find a perch with a commanding view of the target, wait until he's in your sights, and fire. Escape percentages soar with even as scant a lead as five hundred yards on your pursuers. Altogether a preferable modus operandi, and he'd spent half the morning wishing Kliest were around with his tripod rifle. But he wasn't, which left only Wilhelmina. And although he knew its every foible, from its hairtrigger to the way it tended to pull to the left when there was a grain too much powder in the cartridges—something he was able to sense by the second firing—he did not trust the Luger at distances greater than one hundred yards. Even fifty was pushing it. To be absolutely certain Kobelev went down and stayed down, he was going to have to get close, close enough to smell the flesh burn.

At one end of the basement was a door labeled BOILER. This, too, was open, and Carter went in and switched on the light. He had been here earlier with the maintenance man, and it was at that time he'd noticed something peculiar in the construction of these buildings. In the interests of economy the People's Housing Authority had opted for only one central heating system. A massive boiler had been built in the basement of Building "B," large enough to heat the radiators and provide hot water for every unit in the project. This meant that somewhere in the ground between these buildings ran ducts big enough to hold all the necessary plumbing and big enough for a man to pass through in case something had to be repaired.

The boiler room was two stories high, the boiler in the middle taking up almost every inch. Along its bottom, flames danced through the grates of four large furnace doors. It was here Carter had first found the maintenance man. He was gone now, his wheelbarrow and shovel standing in the corner.

A catwalk ringed the room on the second level, leading to a door that stood next to the tunnel down through which pipes were fed. Carter vaulted the railing, ran up the stairs and down the walkway, but when he reached the door, it was locked. Taking out his wallet, he squeezed a narrow, awl-shaped piece of metal out from along the seam and inserted it into the lock. In a few seconds the door swung open, emitting a blast of scorching hot air.

He groped for the light switch but found nothing but rough cement. Repairmen apparently carried lanterns. He put one hand on the railing. It was hot. He stepped inside, feeling his way down the narrow walkway between the pipes and the side of the tunnel, trailing the other hand on the wall.

Something nagged at the back of his mind. Kobelev. How could the man make such a monumental mistake as getting off the train?

TWELVE

On the other side of the utility tunnel, Carter found himself in a basement room. It was lower and larger than the boiler room, lit by a series of narrow windows at ground level. Against the far wall stood a line of washtubs. Half the floor space was given over to parked bicycles.

He took the Luger out and screwed on the silencer, then headed up a crude stairway made of two-by-fours. At the top he opened the thin plywood door a crack and peered into the hallway. A single line of fluorescent tubes illuminated the unremarkable milk white walls and a broken linoleum floor. Along one wall, about the height of a man's thigh, ran a grimy hand streak, and a tricycle lay overturned in a corner. Evidence of children, but there were no children, not even the murmur of their voices. Everything was quiet. Too quiet.

They've cleared the building, Carter thought. *Told everyone to either stay in or get out.*

He edged out into the corridor, snapping off the Luger's safety with his thumb. The old woman's apartment would be dead center on the side facing the street. He moved cautiously in that direction, on tiptoe to keep his shoes from scraping the floor.

He had gone less than fifty feet when a door opened up ahead and two young men stepped into the corridor. Carter quickly ducked into the first available niche and pressed himself against the wall among the mops and buckets.

"When a man breaks his bones and sprains muscles time after time, you have to assume he's doing something wrong," one of them was saying. "Either his technique is bad or he's just clumsy. Janosch may be the greatest goalie in the world, but he's no good to anyone if he doesn't play."

Soccer, Carter thought. *At least they aren't security men.*

The voices came closer. Carter's heart began to race. Fresh droplets of sweat formed on his forehead. He pressed himself flatter against the wall, then looking down, he noticed to his horror that he had pushed one mop and bucket onto its edge, and it was about to topple to the floor. He grabbed it by the mop handle and eased it down on his foot to keep it quiet just as a third voice from somewhere behind the two men said, "Stop."

The two pairs of footsteps suddenly halted, and another set walked a goodly distance down the hall toward them. "This building has been sealed for purposes of state security," the voice said.

Carter peeked around the corner and saw it was one of the goons from the limousine.

"But we are members of the maintenance committee. We have work to do," the young man with opinions on Janosch, the soccer goalie, protested.

"It will not last long," said the KGB man. "Until then, we'd like everyone to stay in and keep these halls clear." His Hungarian was laden with a thick Russian accent. Most likely he was attached to the Soviet embassy, and he and his friend had driven up from Budapest this morning. But where was the other one?

"State security," grumbled the other young man, speaking for the first time. "That's what they said when my father was killed."

"We all have painful memories of the sacrifices the State calls on us to make," the KGB man said. "This is not a big sacrifice today. Spend a few hours at home, read the paper, whatever pleases you. Let us not stir coals that are better left to cool."

Whether it was the reasonableness of the man's tone that convinced them or the familiar bulge in his trench coat pocket, which had not escaped Carter's notice, it was impossible to say, but the three turned and without a further word walked up the hall in the direction from which they'd come, leaving Carter alone in the corridor. A moment later the lights went out, plunging the corridor into darkness, only a small amount of light coming from the end doors.

He waited a few seconds to make sure they'd really gone, then he began moving again, cautiously but quickly, in the direction of Judit Konya's apartment. The speed with which Kobelev's man had intercepted the two in the hall was disturbing. Obviously, not only were they barring people from entering the building, they were keeping a close watch on the interior as well, probably through the small chicken-wired windows at either end of the hall.

He pushed along, his back against the wall, casting a small shadow, until he reached what he considered to be the most likely door. There was no name on it, nothing to distinguish it from any other door facing the hall except it was situated where he thought her apartment should be based on what the maintenance man had told him, and there were small marks along the bottom of the jamb, the kind made by the knock of the steel footrests of a wheelchair when it's not turned short enough.

The door was unlocked. He came through, low and to one side, the Luger in both hands trained on two figures on the other side of the very dark room. One faced him in an old-fashioned wicker wheelchair, the kind used during World War I, a noble-looking woman with features seemingly carved from stone. Her eyes were closed, her head held at an attentive angle as though she were listening, although to what she was listening was not clear except that it was not in this room, or perhaps even of this world. On the wall behind her and to one side hung a crucifix done in the old Hungarian folk style. Myriad votive candles flickered on the table before it, providing what little light there was.

The other figure kneeled in front of her as though praying, the houndstooth coat stretched across his broad back, over the collar a thatch of snow white hair. Kobelev!

He fired twice, the shots slamming Kobelev forward and to

the left. The old woman's eyes sprang open, the knuckle of her left index finger to her mouth.

Carter stood slowly and came toward her, keeping the gun on the body sprawled headlong on the floor. There had been something very peculiar about the way it fell.

He rolled it over with the toe of his shoe. The face was a blank pink cloth stitched in the general proportions of the human countenance. Fleetingly he wondered where the dummy had come from. They certainly hadn't brought it in from the limo.

A noise forced him to turn around. It was one of those sounds that chill the blood several degrees without ever fully registering in the brain, like the rattle of a snake underfoot or the roar of an engine that's too close for comfort. Only in this case it was more muted: the simple metal-on-metal of a hammer drawn back and a cylinder clicked into position.

He started toward the right when a silent tongue of fire lashed out from behind the door. Something sharp and extremely precise, like a power-driven needle, struck his left shoulder and sent him spinning against the wall, knocking over the tables and extinguishing the candles, plunging the room into darkness.

A second silenced shot flashed from the same general location as the first, splintered the table edge, and deflected into the wall a foot or so above Carter's head. Carter fired where he'd seen the light. The bullet whined, glass tinkled, and something heavy hit the floor.

There was dead silence for ten endless seconds, then the very low, agonized moaning of a human being in pain, regular as breathing, like the yawing of a rusty shutter in the wind.

"Yuri?" the old woman queried the darkness.

There was no answer.

"Yuri?"

Carter pulled himself to his feet, his shoulder throbbing with a steady, hot pain, and his fingers growing sticky with blood. He picked up a candle, lit it, and held it up. The flame pulsated to life, and the room's interior became dimly visible. A narrow bed was shoved into a corner, a rustic table beside it served as a nightstand, and above it on the wall were religious pictures of every description. To the left was a doorway that Carter assumed led to some sort of bathroom. The moaning came from inside.

He stepped over with the candle. Lying on the floor, his head supported on one arm draped over the toilet bowl, was one of Kobelev's henchmen. His left eye was a blackened hole from which blood oozed. The other eye stared dumbly at the floor.

Carter turned abruptly and came back across the room toward the old woman. "Who was he?" he hissed at her in Russian.

"You've killed him?" she asked tremulously.

"He's dead."

"My grandson sent him. He told me I needed protection. A man was coming to kill me. Why would you want to kill an old woman like me?" Her head shook as she spoke, whether from fear or old age, Carter couldn't tell.

"Your grandson lied," Carter said. His shoulder hurt like hell. "The other man," he went on, "the one outside. Do you know him?"

"I don't know . . ."

"Call him. Now." He started to push her wheelchair toward the door.

"That's not necessary. You're not Russian."

He thrust the Luger to within a few inches of her face. "Can you feel this?"

Her hands flitted over Wilhelmina's barrel like liver-spotted butterflies. "It's a gun."

"This isn't a matter of choice. You'll do as I say or I'll kill you."

"I'm ninety-three. What makes you think I'm afraid to die?"

"Everyone's afraid to die. Everyone."

Her dry, lined lips broke into a tiny smile. "Hand me my cane." She gestured toward a curved walking stick propped against the end of the bed. Carter fetched it.

Stuffing the Luger back in its holster, he took hold of her arm, which was as light as a dry twig, and eased her forward.

As he did, his gaze was drawn to the floor, to the blank features of the dummy.

If they hadn't brought the dummy with them, he thought, beginning the logical sequence that had been interrupted earlier, then it must have been here to begin with.

She was standing erect now, supporting herself with the cane. "Clear me a path," she snapped. The fear was gone from her voice.

Carter pushed back the table and scraped away the broken glass and candles.

And if it was here all along, then she must have known about it. . . .

She teetered suddenly and he came to her aid, holding her by the elbow and shoulder with his one good arm, and they proceeded together, she taking one tiny step at a time, and he guiding, shoring her up.

And if she knew about it, then she's in on it; and all that bullshit about her life being in danger is just that, bullshit. . . .

Simultaneous with this last thought came the curious sound of metal being drawn across metal, and he became dimly aware she had grown suddenly stronger in his grasp. Abruptly she pulled away from him, and for a brief instant he stared in wonderment, amazed at how well she stood without his help. In the same instant he saw a flash above her head like light glinting off a blade, and he realized suddenly the walking stick had disappeared. He jumped back in barely enough time to avoid being run through by her initial thrust. The sword grazed his lower abdomen and opened an oblong slash in his shirt. He grabbed her wrist, twisted, and the blade clattered to the floor. He pushed her roughly toward the door, which he eased open a few inches.

He held the Luger against her back as she stuck her head out and called down the hall.

"Comrade Tremloff!"

They waited several seconds.

"Louder," Carter urged.

"Comrade Tremloff!"

The door at the end of the hall clicked open, then wedged shut, and footsteps came quickly down the linoleum. "Yes, Madam Konya?"

"Invite him in," Carter whispered.

"One of the candles has fallen to the floor and I fear a fire, Comrade," she said.

"Where is Yuri? Can't he help?"

He never received an answer. As he spoke he edged in through the door, exposing a long pink oval of scalp to Carter's waiting gun butt. Carter swung, and the man sank heavily to the floor. Carter rolled him over and extracted his revolver from the holster under his arm. It was a Graz-Buyra, identical to the one he'd taken off another flunkie named Mandaladov in an airport washroom in Phoenix. "Must be the gun of the day in Kobelev's private army," he muttered, but the thought struck him that he had not seen this man on the train, which meant he was probably stationed here in Hungary, another link in Kobelev's vast network that seemed to reach everywhere.

"You will run now like a dog to save your skin, but it is too late," the old woman said above him.

"My skin and others'," he replied.

"My grandson will kill you," she said resolutely.

"One of us will die, that much is certain."

"He will hunt you on every continent after what you did to my poor great-granddaughter."

"I don't have time to argue," said Carter, unloading the big Russian's automatic and pocketing the shells. He tossed the gun aside.

"Crippling a girl in the prime of her life before she's had a chance to bear children. . ."

Carter ignored her. He glanced around the room. It had been nothing more than an elaborate trap. He brushed past the old woman and hurried out the door.

"She was beautiful," she shouted after him, her words ringing in the narrow hall. "The cream of Russian manhood sought her in every capital of the world, and now she must live in a wheelchair like a dried, juiceless old crone!"

Outside he walked quickly to the Fiat and climbed in. As he started the engine, a bright silver gash appeared on the hood.

Turning, Carter saw another of Kobelev's bodyguards crouched by the building entrance, his gun out in front of him and a pale ghost of barrel smoke disappearing over his shoulder.

Carter gunned it. The car jerked forward, and the second shot missed.

He took the first corner standing on the accelerator. The rear wheels skidded crazily, and he ripped out a kiosk on the far side of the street. The little engine had more power than he thought. By the time he'd gotten himself righted and into third gear, he was doing better than sixty.

Side streets flew by at a dizzying rate. He looked frantically down each one, trying to find a likely route to the train station, but each of them was choked with horse-drawn carriages and carts. It was as though the whole of Hungarian peasantry had come to the city for a Sunday visit.

He came to an intersection marked with an international stop sign, ignored it, cranked the wheel to the left with his one good arm, and narrowly missed a knot of pedestrians in front of a café. A military-type van swerved to avoid a collision, and its several passengers glared at him from its windows.

He careened down three more blocks, spotted a likely alley, turned into it, and stopped. Rolling down the window, he listened anxiously. Nothing. Just the motor ticking under the hood. He listened for another thirty seconds, longer than he dared, and still nothing. No sirens, no screaming engines in pursuit. He started the car again, put it into gear, and drove much more slowly down the street.

He had lost the way to the train station. He had a feeling it lay further in the direction he'd been traveling when he first left the housing project, but he wasn't certain, and it was too dangerous to return that way to see. He would just have to wend his way through the lesser-used back roads and alleys and hope he chanced on it soon.

He turned into a promising-looking thoroughfare, but it

soon reduced itself to a wagon rut that disappeared into someone's vegetable plot. Another street was blocked by a peasant's wagon hitched to an obstinate workhorse. The horse's master, a quarrelsome old man with no teeth, seemed in no hurry to move him, and it took several minutes of honking before two other men, obviously relatives, came out from one of the buildings, and amid much shouting and gesturing, finally convinced the old-timer to clear the way.

A half dozen blocks back the way he had come, he turned a corner and suddenly was there. He pulled into a parking spot several hundred yards from the station's entrance, got out, and went into a café across the street. Roberta was to have been waiting for him at the table by the window. The place, however, was deserted.

A short husky man wearing an apron came from the back.

"There was a girl here," Carter said.

The man stopped in his tracks and stared open-mouthed at Carter.

"The girl," Carter said, looking over his shoulder out at the street and across at the station behind which the Orient Express had been waiting. But it was pulling out now. It was leaving!

A black sedan jerked to a stop across the street. Its door swung open, and a young woman got out and rushed around the station, running after the departing train.

Someone aboard the train had opened a door, and hands reached down to help the running woman swing aboard.

But even from where Carter was standing, there had been no mistaking that graceful, athletic young figure. It had been Tatiana Kobelev, one hundred percent restored.

THIRTEEN

The scenery rushed at him through the Fiat's windshield, a kaleidoscope of shapes and colors without definition. He squinted into the sun, clinging to the wheel with his good arm, desperately fighting to stay conscious. The pain was no longer centered in his shoulder. It had spread throughout his body, and with each beat of his heart, his whole being seemed to throb.

The flat, monotonous fields outside Györ had given way to the rounded crests of the Transdanubian Mountains, and the driving was getting more difficult. The road dropped three or four hundred feet in the space of half a mile, then rose almost as quickly in short, unexpected curves. More than once Carter jerked awake to find himself on the wrong side of the white line, another vehicle bearing down on him.

He knew he needed doctoring and needed it fast. He had ignored the awesome pain in his ribs after his fight with Shurin, and it had eventually subsided. There wasn't much one could do with cracked ribs but tape them and let them heal. But a bullet wound was a different matter.

And yet whenever he thought about the pain, which was every few seconds, his foot only pressed harder on the accelerator.

He had lost sight of the train in the intricate byways of Györ but relocated it again several times out on the flats, its stack spitting out black coal smoke as it charged down the track under a full head of steam. Running parallel with it at times, it galled him to think Cynthia and Roberta were only a few hundred feet away yet impossible to get to. It galled him, too, to think Kobelev and his daughter were together again, and there was nothing preventing him from killing Cynthia and even Roberta anytime he wanted.

He'd lost track of the train again during its ascent into the mountains, and by now he hadn't seen it for almost thirty minutes. His only hope, he figured, was by some miracle to meet the train in Budapest ninety kilometers away. It would stop if only for coal and water, and he had to be there when it did.

For the thousandth time he rubbed his eyes and willed himself to stay conscious and forget about the pain, and for the thousandth time his body answered with a constant hum, a "white noise" of red-hot sensation. The white line began to waiver in front of the hood. Soon it was further to the right than it was to the left. A car hurled itself at him from the opposite direction, its horn screaming a warning. He twisted the wheel at the last minute and it sped past, its angry wail fading gradually behind him.

This time it had been too close for comfort. He pulled over to the shoulder and stopped, his knuckles white on the steering wheel, his heart galloping in his chest. There was nothing he could do, no way to get help. He forced his mind through every possibility from calling Hawk and having him send out the militia, to giving up right here and now and curling up to die, but nothing was viable. In the end there was only one course and that was to do what he was doing. He started the engine and pulled out onto the asphalt, wondering if he would wake up in time the next time.

Within a few minutes, despite his resolve, his eyelids began to droop and then close. In a few seconds he heard a rapping against the right front fender as though someone were hitting it with a hammer. He jumped awake in time to see the boulders on the road shoulder close enough in the passenger window to pick out the grain in the rock. He tried to pull away, but the bouncing against the granite wall jerked the steering wheel from his hand. The car caught a particularly large outcropping, spun around, and came to a sudden halt, throwing Carter against the door shoulder first. The pain exploded in his arm like a fragmentation grenade. He made only the briefest pass at staying awake before black night overtook him.

An old peasant woman carrying a steaming basin of water in her arms peered at him shrewdly from a distance of less than a foot, then turned and waddled across the low-ceilinged, whitewashed room to a boy who sat by a crude wood-burning stove. She poured the water from the basin into the sink and without looking at the boy, told him, "Fetch the doctor. The American is awake."

In less than a minute the boy returned with a swarthy man in his mid-fifties, a thick salt-and-pepper mustache covering his upper lip and his shirt-sleeves rolled up. Encircling his eyes were a pair of wire-rimmed glasses, over the tops of which he gave Carter a studious look. "How are you feeling?" he asked in English. "You are American?"

"Shaky," Carter said, ignoring the second question.

"You've had quite an ordeal. I took this out of your shoulder last night." He held up a wad of blood-encrusted lead.

"Last night? What day is it?"

"Monday."

"Holy Christ!" said Carter, starting to get up.

"Easy," said the doctor, holding him with a firm grip on his arm and shoulder. "You're not in any shape to go anywhere just yet. You'll have that wound open if you persist."

"You don't understand! I have to be in Budapest! I was supposed to be there yesterday!"

Carter struggled against the doctor's hold on him, the effort playing havoc with his shoulder.

"Go!" the doctor shouted to the boy who had been watching just inside the door. "Tell the commandant I can't hold him."

Carter strained for a few minutes more, then fell back on the bed exhausted. "They're gone by now, anyway," he mumbled.

"You are quite right, my friend," said a low, cultured voice. Both Carter and the doctor turned around. In the doorway, filling it, was a tall, elegantly slim man in the blue serge uniform of the Hungarian People's Army. At least it looked like other Hungarian Army uniforms Carter had seen; the difference was this one didn't fit like a gunny sack. It had been custom tailored to smooth out every bulge and wrinkle. From the gold on his shoulders, Carter guessed a colonel or higher.

"Let him up, Doctor, if he wants to sit."

The doctor released him, and Carter pulled himself painfully into a position where he could lean his back on the whitewashed wall.

"The doctor tells me you have remarkable powers of recovery," the commandant said, coming closer. "I see now that he was right. Most admirable. Would you care for a cigarette?" He held out a gold case filled with dark brown cigarettes, which Carter recognized as Russian-made. Carter took one, then the commandant took out one for himself, tapped it firmly against the case, and lit it. He lit Carter's, then drew up a chair and sat down.

"Where am I?" asked Carter.

"In the mountains about halfway between Budapest and Györ. The village is called Diosd. One of the local peasants found you after your unfortunate accident while he was returning home from making a delivery. He was going to take you to the hospital in Budapest, but he recognized a bullet wound when he saw one and figured you were in some sort of trouble, so he brought you here."

"Some favor," said Carter sourly.

The commandant smiled. "You mustn't blame the peasant for my presence. He had no choice in that. Besides, I'm afraid you overestimate the effectiveness of your security. We've been monitoring your movements since you left Györ. We would have found you after you failed to pass through our last checkpoint, in any event. And after all, it isn't so bad, is it? Your wound has been tended to, and soon you will be given free transportation back to the Austrian border."

"I have a job to finish in Budapest."

"Doctor, would you excuse us for a moment?" asked the commandant.

The doctor raised an eyebrow, then without a word walked to the sink, gathered up several instruments that lay in a tray beside it, and went out the door.

When he was gone, the commandant pulled his chair several feet closer to the bed. "I think you should know," he said in a confidential tone, "my superiors regard you as nothing more than a common assassin and would like to have you shot. And they would have sent me here to do just that if it weren't for the Soviets themselves. None of them seems to be able to determine where Comrade Kobelev stands in the pecking order. They are afraid to serve his cause and afraid not to. They are very confused, and as long as they remain so, we Hungarians will wash our hands of both of you. Kobelev is speeding out of the country right now, and you are incapacitated. Things work out well in the end, no?"

"No," said Carter resolutely. "There are two women aboard that train, American citizens, and my government is going to take it very much amiss if any harm—"

"Ach!" the commandant exclaimed harshly. "You have no rights here. You have all entered the country illegally. All except Miss Stewart, which I am told is her real name, and she is nothing but a spy masquerading as a Hungarian schoolteacher. You are all undesirable aliens, and we shall be glad to get rid of the lot of you!" He punctuated this last statement by snapping the ash from his cigarette onto the immaculate wooden floor, and for several minutes this ended the conversation.

They smoked. The commandant watched Carter, but Carter ignored him and stared at the floor. He was thinking of Cynthia and Roberta and his dwindling chances of rescuing them.

"You know," said the commandant finally, "it isn't that I dislike you, my friend. You are an impressive man, and I must admire your training. For instance, your Hungarian is very good, almost accent-free. And you have come a long way against formidable odds. The doctor tells me you've had several ribs cracked recently. Your capacity for punishment is astonishing. But I have a job to do."

"You don't like Kobelev any better than I do, do you?" asked Carter.

"What makes you say that?"

"It's true, isn't it?"

"I dislike the man, I'll admit it. He's a legend in the KGB. The stories they tell are frightening. Let me put it this way—I disapprove of his methods. To me he typifies the entire Soviet approach to government. Ruthless, power-for-the-sake-of-power. Altogether a despicable man. But one can't always choose one's bed partners in this day and age. A small country such as mine must be aligned with someone strong."

Outside, an engine started up. "What's that?" asked Carter.

"The helicopter to take you to Austria. I imagine a man of your extraordinary endurance is up to traveling."

The door swung open and the doctor rushed in. His hair was windblown, and behind him out in the barnyard the grass was being whipped flat by the wash from the chopper's big rotor.

"You can't move this man now!" he shouted.

"Why not?" asked the commandant calmly.

"Because his condition hasn't had a chance to stabilize. Move him now and you may kill him."

"Orders are orders, Doctor. I'm afraid our friend here is something of an embarrassment."

"You let me save his life. You don't expect me to stand by and let you kill him, do you? Give him twenty-four hours."

The commandant slowly shook his head.

"We are not like these Americans who believe in nothing but money. We have some appreciation for the value of a human life."

The commandant looked hard at Carter, considering. Finally he said, "Very well. Twenty-four hours. No longer. I'll leave the helicopter and crew on hand to take him back as soon as you say he's up to it." He opened the door, then turned and looked directly at Carter. "We are not barbarians," he said and went out.

The doctor came over and gently took the cigarette from

Carter's fingers and dropped it with a hiss in a nearby water glass. "You must sleep," he said. "You'll need your strength."

"Can't I make anyone understand?" asked Carter plaintively. "The lives of two young women depend on—"

"Shh!" said the doctor harshly. "Sleep. I've bought you some time. Hopefully enough to keep you alive. Don't ruin it by trying to do something foolish."

He pushed Carter back on the bed and pulled the blanket up under his chin. Carter stopped fighting. He was afraid the doctor would give him something to make him sleep, and he needed his thinking sharp. The doctor pulled the crude homespun curtains over the low windows and crept to the door. He opened it, creating an oblong of light, and stepped out. Behind him, staring in, wide-eyed, was the boy.

When Carter's eyelids next fluttered open, he found himself surrounded by a pale yellow light. The boy was standing over him holding up a chimneyless kerosene lantern and staring. When he realized Carter was awake, he gave a little gasp of fright.

"Don't be scared," Carter whispered. "What's your name?"

"Milos," the boy replied softly.

"Milos. Ever been to Budapest, Milos?"

The boy nodded.

"I'll bet you'd like to live there someday."

The boy nodded again, vigorously.

"I'd like to get to Budapest, Milos. I have some friends there waiting for me. But these men won't let me go. I have to go, and they won't let me. I need help, Milos. Your help, if I'm ever going to get there in time. Do you like knives, Milos?"

The boy nodded again and produced an ancient jackknife from his pocket. It was Swiss but had been badly abused by one of its owners. Only two blades remained, one of them rusty and the other badly chipped. And yet, in the way he handled it, Carter could see it was worth its weight in gold to the boy.

"I'll bet no one else around here has a knife as nice as this." He took it from the boy and held it up to look at it. "Two blades," he said appreciatively, pulling out the rusty one and running his finger along its edge. "Where did you get it?"

"Traded for it," said the boy.

Carter nodded sagely. "I have a knife, too," he said, "even nicer than this. I'd be willing to give it to someone who helped me get to Budapest."

The boy said nothing.

Carter took him earnestly by the arm. "My clothes, Milos. And my weapons. The soldiers have them outside. Bring them to me and I'll give you as fine a knife as you've ever seen, I promise you."

The boy's gaze remained level, and Carter wasn't sure he'd understood. He thought of rephrasing it somehow but decided it was no use. Wilhelmina and Hugo were most likely locked away in a police vault miles from here by now. He fell back on the bed and sighed. The boy reached over, retrieved his knife, and put it back in his pocket.

The door swung open suddenly, and the peasant woman appeared with a bucket in her hand. "Milos!" she shouted. "Get away from there!"

The boy backed away guiltily.

"Go on now. Go out and play. Leave the poor man alone." She flapped her apron at him as though she were herding chickens. The boy hurried to the door, opened it, but before going out he cast a hasty glance back at Carter. Then he ran off, and the woman slammed the door behind him. "Ruffian," she exclaimed, shaking her head when he was gone.

She turned and poured the contents of the bucket into a large kettle on the stove. Then with a long match she lit a fire and fed it wood a few pieces at a time. There was something in her movements, the slow, ponderous way she worked, that was relaxing to watch. When the kettle was steaming, she picked it off the stove and brought it over beside the bed. "I have to change those dressings," she said.

Slowly she began to undo the gauze bandage the doctor

had put on earlier. The wound looked ugly, but her calm, purposeful expression never changed. Gently she dabbed at his shoulder with cotton and water from the kettle. "I'm the horse doctor around here," she said. "That's why they brought you to me. Show me a body can mend a horse, and I'll show you a body can fix almost anything." Her country accent had a delightful lilt.

When she finished cleaning the area, she snipped off several lengths of gauze and tenderly pressed them into place. Then she taped him. When she was done she told Carter to roll onto his stomach.

For several minutes her strong fingers kneaded the muscles of his shoulder and neck in a slow steady rhythm, then Carter lost track of the individual movements and gave himself over to the overall sensation of pleasure. The effect was miraculous. Pain and tension seemed to melt away. He relaxed completely and was soon fast asleep.

He awoke the second time in darkness. There was no light at the window or at the threshold of the door. At first he thought he was alone, then he heard a movement. Shoes shuffled across the wooden floor. Something heavy landed on the foot of the bed. Pulling himself up, he reached down to feel what it was. Wilhelmina.

"Milos?"

In answer, something else fell, this time lighter and more flexible. He ran his hand down and felt the rough shirt and trousers Schwetzler had lent him what now seemed like years ago.

"Good work, Milos, my boy!"

Carter got up and hastily began to dress. He was a bit shaky but too excited to care. He pulled on the trousers as best he could and was tucking in the shirttail when the boy struck a match and lit the kerosene lamp. When he had it flickering, he sat down in a chair and began to examine the stiletto, lovingly running his fingers up and down the blade.

"That's right. She's all yours, Milos," Carter whispered, checking the Luger's cartridge clip, then stuffing it into the waistband of his trousers. "Here, let me show you something." He came over, picked up Hugo's special sheath, and fastened it to the boy's forearm. Then he loaded the stiletto into the spring mechanism. "Now flex the muscle," he said. The boy flexed, and the knife shot out and skidded across the floor. The boy started to retrieve it when Carter caught him by the arm and spun him around until they were looking directly into one another's eyes.

"This is no toy, son. It's a weapon used to kill men. More than one has left his blood on it. Think about that and treat it accordingly." The boy nodded solemnly.

While Milos was on the other side of the room, Carter bent down and blew out the lantern. The boy seemed to sense what was happening and stopped moving.

Carter drew back the window curtain. The helicopter's long blades glistened in the moonlight. To the left, in the shadow of a low, oblong shed, the flames of a small fire danced in the wind. He started for the door, but the boy grabbed his arm. "So long," Carter said in English, squeezing the boy's shoulder. "You'd better hide that knife for a while, or they're going to know who helped me out of here."

For a moment the boy just held him as though he wanted to say something but was having trouble finding the words. Then he said, "*Koszonom.*"

"You're welcome," said Carter, ruffling the boy's hair. Then he pushed open the wooden door as noiselessly as he could and descended into the barnyard.

The helicopter stood on a grassy plot between the house and the shed, a Soviet production model, the kind the NATO boys called a "hound." It was easy to see why the doctor had been reluctant to have him moved in it. In this particular version the passenger capsule had been removed and the after-cabin left open. It would be cold and breezy at five thousand feet.

He crept along the stock fence to the far side of the shed, to the end opposite the glowing fire, then through the thick grass along the shed's outer wall until he was close enough to see the long shadows the men cast and hear their voices.

Silently he flipped off the Luger's safety, then crouched down to wait. Bits of conversation came to him on the wind, but nothing coherent. Then he heard the dry weeds crackle a few yards off, and he knew it wouldn't be long.

A dark figure appeared around the corner of the building, unzipped his pants and spread his legs slightly. A soft hissing followed as Carter stole up from behind.

"Not a movement, not a sound," he whispered as he placed the Luger's barrel to the back of the man's head. The man stiffened, and his stream abruptly terminated. "You're through here. Turn around and walk back to your friends."

As they entered the firelight, the conversation suddenly stopped, the others turning toward them.

"Throw your guns down," Carter shouted. The men obeyed. There were two AK-47 machine guns and several small arms.

When they were disarmed, Carter motioned for them to stand, then waved them away from the helicopter. "Turn around and start walking away. Now! Move it."

For a moment or two it seemed as if the soldiers would not obey his commands. He raised his weapon a little higher, and they turned and hurried away.

He let them get at least a hundred yards away before he scrambled aboard the chopper.

The machine started easily, and in a moment or two the oil pressure had come up, and the engine steadied. The soldiers were running toward the house. Probably more weapons.

Carefully Carter eased the pitch and speed controls forward, and the machine slowly lifted off the ground, the pain from his wound making him nauseated. But he was on his way, the thought of Kobelev blanking out all other considerations.

Budapest with its geometric grid of lights and black Danubian abyss in its center came and went, as did the local air traffic control, whom Carter managed to convince he was on an important military exercise. Word had evidently not caught up with him yet.

From the charts aboard, Carter figured Kobelev and the kidnapped train had passed Budapest hours ago. By now it would be nearly to the Rumanian border to the south.

South of the city he picked up the mainline tracks, dipped in low, and cranked the throttle full.

The land flattened, and the tracks ran like knife edges toward the horizon. He kept his altitude low, rising only for bridges and overhead wires.

Within half an hour he had reached Szolnok on the Tisza River. He skirted the town and continued south, the steady beat of the rotors almost lulling him to sleep. It seemed as if he had been flying forever, toward a goal he would never reach . . . out of touch with the world and with his own past, Kobelev the only thought that mattered any longer.

FOURTEEN

Carter crossed into Rumania in the twilight just before dawn. The ground elevation had risen sharply in the last hour and a half, and as the first shafts of light struck the terrain, it wasn't sand and grass that turned pink, it was snow. This was mountain country. To the east and south stood the Carpathians and the Transylvanian Alps, floating on the horizon like huge ships. Towering in the center, old Moldoveanu herself, rising to a height of over eight thousand feet, was visible even though the peak was more than seventy miles away.

The track began to rise, too, winding in and out of valleys, hugging the mountainsides, a speckled band of black dirt and gleaming steel against the whitened rock. Carter followed it relentlessly. His arm ached terribly, and he estimated he'd come almost two hundred miles, but there was still no sign of the kidnapped train.

Worried thoughts began to haunt him: maybe he'd taken the wrong set of tracks; maybe they'd stopped somewhere along the way and he'd missed them; or maybe they'd gone south from Budapest to Belgrade instead.

His fuel was getting low. If he went much further, he'd crash out here and be stranded in the snow and wind.

He'd almost convinced himself to give up and turn around when he saw a telltale plume of black smoke hanging in the air opposite a curve. He rounded the breast of land and there she was, steaming for all she was worth, engine black as night, pushrods pumping, billows of coal smoke streaming out of her stack. Behind her followed the fifteen antique cars, each painted slightly differently, making her look at first glance like some sort of a show train.

He swung to the right and pulled back around the edge of the mountain, not wanting to be seen. This was going to take some strategy. He pulled up on the collective pitch and immediately gained altitude, although he realized there was a limit as to how high he could go. The air here was colder and drier than it had been the night before, which meant it wouldn't work as well in the rotors. Also, he was going to have to consume more fuel to go the same distance.

He flew over a low peak and descended into the valley on the other side, then found the track again and followed it for another two miles. By this time he figured he'd gained fifteen minutes on the train and began to circle, searching the mountain for a particular type of snow formation, one that bulged conspicuously at the bottom of its shelf.

He found what he was looking for hanging well above the track, and he made a pass at it, coming in very close, the sharp *chop-chop* of the rotor blades reverberating within the narrow cut of the valley.

A clot of coal smoke appeared around the curve below.

Carter made a second pass, the sweat beginning to bead on his forehead as he cranked the throttle full forward. Again the tremendous din of the helicopter engine and rotors hammering at the snow shelf.

The train steamed into view at the bottom of the long grade as Carter maneuvered the helicopter up and around in a gut-wrenching tight curve, and the snow began to slide off the side of the mountain, slowly at first, then faster and faster, covering the tracks.

The train was already slowing down as Carter lifted the stick and disappeared over the summit. He flew down into the preceding valley, found a convenient flat spot, and landed.

In the nose he found a heavy parka and a medical kit. He stripped off his shirt and looked at his wound. The doctor had done a pretty good job. The stitches looked as though they'd hold, except liquid had begun to form around the ends of the black thread, a bad sign. Fortunately it had gotten so cold during the course of the night that it was too numb to hurt much.

He rebandaged the wound, then put his shirt back on. He pulled on the parka and checked Wilhelmina. There were only nine cartridges left in the Luger. He stuffed it into one of the coat's big side pockets and climbed out into the snow. The sun was just coming over the horizon.

Carter trotted up the tracks. Ahead, a cloud of vapor billowed from around the curve, and the air was full of the hiss of escaping steam. He ducked behind a series of boulders alongside the track and proceeded from one to the next until he was able to see the rear of the train.

Two of Kobelev's guards stood on the small railed platform at the end of the last car, each with a light machine gun slung over his shoulder. They were dressed in furs and leather like two Sherpa mountain guides and were laughing. The words were garbled, but the tone was unmistakable. Obviously, they'd come prepared for the weather.

Carter was going to have to take them both out, but in such a way that neither of them fired a shot. One burst from those machine guns and the whole train would come running. The last thing he needed at this point was a shoot-out.

He moved up behind another boulder until he was within fifty yards, the furthest he could be and still be dead certain of his marksmanship. Then he leaned forward, screwed the silencer on the end of the barrel, steadied his hand on the rock, and waited.

The two men continued to talk and laugh. One seemed to be telling the other a story. Occasionally, disjointed shouts floated to Carter from the front of the train, and every so often he had to put his gun down and blow on his fingers to keep them from freezing.

Finally the one guard reached the punchline, and the other man laughed heartily while the first turned his head out of the wind to light a cigarette.

This was the moment Carter had been waiting for. He aimed at the laughing man, gently squeezed, and put the bullet into the back of his throat. The guard's head slammed against the back of the car, bounced forward, and he ended up folded over the low railing.

The second man looked up, the cigarette falling from his mouth. In his astonishment the whites of his eyes were visible even at fifty yards. Carter put his second shot in the man's neck behind his left ear. The bullet blew out part of the man's head, spraying blood for several feet. He fell onto the first man, then slumped to the floor, his body twitching.

Carter ran to the train, relieved both men of their machine guns, flinging one as far as he could into the valley below and shouldering the other, then he entered the car. It was empty. These were servants' quarters, tight little berths with no more than a pull-down bed and a window, but none of the beds was pulled down, and each of the narrow sliding doors stood open. There was no sign anyone had been in here recently.

He went on to the next car—a sleeping car with old-fashioned upholstered seats. It was empty as well. A small heater at the end of the aisle was blowing out warm air. He stooped to warm his hands, listening. There wasn't a sound; the train seemed deserted. He wondered if the passengers hadn't gotten off somewhere along the way.

He went on to the next car. More berths, although these were for the paying customers, bigger than those earlier and better appointed, with tasseled curtains and small porcelain basins for washing along one wall. Carter eased up the passageway, looking into each compartment with the machine gun at the ready, no longer sure what to expect.

"Nick?" someone whispered behind him. He spun around. Roberta, her hair disheveled, her eyes brimming with relief, ran to him and buried her face in his good shoulder.

He let her cry for a moment, then pulled away. "Get yourself together," he told her.

"I could have taken him," she said with sudden force. "But my gun jammed.

"They kicked all the passengers and crew off in Budapest. Not that any of them were too sorry to leave. But Tatiana is back!"

"I saw her getting on the train at Györ. Where's Cynthia?"

"Up front. Second car back from the engine."

"She's still alive?"

Roberta nodded. "I was just so relieved to see you. When they stopped because of the avalanche, I thought I'd die here. And then it occurred to me that it might be you. I didn't believe it, but thank God I was right. What the hell happened to your arm?"

"Little problem in Györ. Our friend Kobelev is always thinking. He figured I might remember his grandmother, so he laid a trap for me. Damn near worked."

She unzipped the parka and unbuttoned his shirt. "Oh, Nick!" she exclaimed when she saw it. "You need help."

"Later."

Her eyes danced away from his, out across the car, the lids batting back tears. "I made a mistake, Nick. I'm sorry. I guess because you're a man you get to be the big hero. At any rate, when I got here I realized there wasn't much I could do, so I lay low. Last night when everyone was asleep, I thought I'd take a chance. I crept into the salon car up front and found Kobelev sleeping, unguarded for the moment. I had the drop on him, but then my damn gun jammed. I just made it out of there."

"You were lucky you weren't captured, too."

"You know something, Carter?" she asked indignantly, her shame turning to anger at last. "Throughout our entire association you have given me absolutely no credit whatsoever. When you first met me, you mistook me for a whore, then you shuffled me down to the train station to wait like a little girl while you went to intercept Kobelev at his grandmother's. Now you tell me you don't think I'm capable of a simple operation of the kind I've been trained to do."

"All right," he said, trying to calm her. "I apologize, too. I made a mistake in Austria, and I should have taken you with me in Györ. I could have used you. So now we're even. Let's bury the hatchet. We don't have time to squabble among ourselves."

"I'll forgive you if you promise an apology in full when all this is over."

"Done. Now let's go find Kobelev."

They worked their way through the remaining cars of the train, the pullmans, the sleeping cars, a shower car, the dining car, and the kitchen where Nick had fought Shurin; all were deserted. When they reached the small salon car where Carter had had his initial confrontation with Kobelev, they conferred quietly outside the door.

"Last time I was here," Carter whispered, "there were two guards, one at this end and one at the other."

"Same as last night," Roberta said.

"Then we'll have to assume they're still in there. You go back a car, get off the train, then walk up to the other end of this car, being careful not to let anybody see you. Then we go in together. I'll rush this door and take out the first guard. You rush the other door and draw the second's attention. With the first guard out of the way, we'll have him in a crossfire. But don't shoot unless you absolutely have to. We still don't know if Kobelev is in there, and I'd rather not advertise the fact his support troops have dwindled down to almost nothing."

Roberta nodded, taking the light machine gun Carter offered her. They synchronized watches. "Five minutes," he said.

"You sure you trust me not to screw this up?" she asked.

"Get out of here! Let's not start that whole thing again!" She turned and slipped out of the car.

Carter watched the digital display on his wrist until the five minutes had elapsed, then burst in the door at the exact moment Roberta shouldered her way in at the other side. The car was empty.

"They've been here," said Roberta. "Here's Kobelev's pipe. It's still warm."

"And Cynthia's wheelchair. At least they're letting her up. But where the hell is everybody?"

"Outside I heard voices at the front of the train."

"Let's have a look."

They went through a club car similar to the one they'd just left, except it had no bar. It, too, was empty, although it had been recently occupied. The following car was the coal tender, which they climbed over to get to the engine compartment. This was also deserted, even though the fire doors stood open and a fierce coal fire glowed inside.

The voices were clearly audible now, and Carter thought he recognized Kobelev's. He leaned out the engineer's window and saw the Russian standing in front of the engine, his hands on his hips, his white hair pressed down by a thick fur *addyel*. He was watching two of his guards, the engineer, and the fireman all plying coal shovels to the mound of snow that blocked the track. He was shouting orders, admonishing them to dig faster. Beside him stood a slender woman with black hair. She looked at first like Tatiana, but he guessed it must be Cynthia because under the man's overcoat that hung from her shoulders like a tent, she seemed to be wearing nothing more than a robe and nightgown.

He leaned a little further out the opening and leveled the Luger at the Russian.

He was just about to pull the trigger when a bullet ricocheted off the side of the engine, inches from his hand.

Carter ducked back out of sight, Roberta by his side. "Where is he?" she asked.

"Above us. Somewhere forward."

She popped up, took a quick look, and fired a short burst from the machine gun. Her shots were quickly answered with an equally short burst that sent bullets whining off the walls of the compartment.

"You all right?" she asked, crouching down again and looking at Carter's hand, which he was shaking as though he'd been stung.

"Just metal splinters. Dammit! I should have realized. He posted guards in the rear because he thought I had something to do with the avalanche. Of course he'd post another above the train to keep an eye on the whole thing in case I got by the first two."

There were more shots, this time from the other side and lower, coming up through the space between the coal tender and the engine, putting deep silver marks in the boilerplate just over their heads.

"Carter!" came a shout from the direction of the second set of shots. "I hope you weren't intending to run away with my train. Thanks to you, it isn't going anywhere."

"Neither are you, Kobelev!" Carter shouted back.

There was more firing, this time from both directions at once, and Carter and Roberta huddled in a corner so as not to be caught by a ricochet.

"Give yourselves up!" shouted Kobelev. "We have you pinned down. Besides, we still have your friend."

"But we have the train!" retorted Carter. He crawled through the coal dust on the floor and peeked out at Kobelev's position. They were using the large boulders the avalanche had kicked down for cover. He rattled off two shots that made heads duck. The answering volley came from the guard on the other side, ringing off the metal floor and kicking up coal dust on all sides of him. He barely managed to roll toward the fire doors for safety.

Roberta slid over and put a hand on his leg. "What are we going to do?"

Carter took a quick look around the cab. It was an old engine, manufactured in Germany probably before the turn of the century. The German labels for the different handles and gauges had long since worn off, but the controls looked simple.

"If worst comes to worst," he said, "we can back out of here, although it'd be tough on these grades. But the way I see it now, it's a stand-off. We'll just sit and wait."

"What if they rush us?"

"How much ammunition have you got?"

She checked the machine gun's magazine. "Thirty—maybe forty rounds," she announced, slamming it back into place.

"We can hold them. They may have the numbers, but we've got the fire. They're stuck out in the cold."

• • •

But the cold didn't remain cold. As the day wore on, the sun outside grew warmer while the fire under the boiler grew cooler. And with the area between the tender and the engine a no-man's-land of crossfire, Carter was unable to get to the coal. The fire went from red hot to smokey gray and finally, by midafternoon, to speckled black embers with streaks of red beneath the ash—far too low to get up steam if they needed to make a quick exit.

The lengthening shadows toward evening found Carter and Roberta huddling in front of the furnace for warmth, one watching one door, one watching the other. It had been a long day, filled with shouts and threats and even an occasional shot being fired, but nothing was resolved.

"I'm hungry," Roberta said at last.

"It's hard to be cold on an empty stomach," Carter said. He was thinking about Cynthia. He hoped Kobelev had provisions out there.

"I'm still hungry."

"Wait a minute," said Carter, noticing the familiar shape of a black metal box stashed under the driver's seat. He slid toward it, and a shot hit the seat back, making it ring like a gong. He snatched the box and beat a hasty retreat.

"It looks like a lunch box," Roberta said excitedly.

Carter popped it open. Inside were four stale hot-cross buns, some waxed wrapping from buns already eaten, and a half a thermos of tepid coffee. The driver had a sweet tooth.

With the coming of darkness coal became easier to obtain. Carter made the trip between tender and engine several times without being fired upon, and soon the cabin was warm enough to allow them to undo their coats. Roberta searched through the lockers opposite the driver's and found a fire ax, a box of flares and a medical kit. She promptly set to work changing the dressing on Carter's shoulder, while Carter sat with the machine gun on his knee watching both exposures.

"How long are we going to have to stay here like this?" she finally asked.

Carter looked up at her and shrugged. "I don't know. It's up to them, really." He laid the weapon aside. Roberta had repacked the first-aid kit, and she sat on her haunches looking at him, their faces very close.

Slowly Carter leaned toward her, then stopped. Her nostrils flared, and it seemed like she would bolt at any moment.

"What's the matter?" he asked.

She glanced outside. "Do you love her?"

"Who?" Carter asked, genuinely confused.

"Cynthia."

"No," he said. "We're good friends, that's all."

"Oh," Roberta said, and she was in his arms, careful not to press against his wound, and they were kissing, her lips soft, warm and moist.

They parted and she quickly pulled her sweater and turtleneck off, then undid her bra, her breasts firm and high, her nipples already hard. She pulled off her boots and trousers as Carter quickly got undressed, and soon they were lying nude in each other's arms in front of the warm firebox.

"This is crazy," Carter said. "Kobelev could decide to send his people in here at any moment."

"I know," Roberta said, gulping her words. "But it's been so . . . long. . ."

"Shut up, Lieutenant Commander," Carter said gently. She lay back as he kissed her breasts, then worked his way down her flat stomach, and lower, all else forgotten for the moment.

Much later the stars appeared in the oblong of sky between the cabin's roof and the top of the coal tender, and the wind picked up. Carter noticed the pressure had pushed the boiler near the danger point. He fumbled with the various valves and spigots, squinting at the faded German instructions in the dark until he finally located one he thought would do the trick and opened it, slowly at first. Steam billowed out of the big tank with a hiss that bordered on a full-throated scream, filling the cabin with the moist stench of rusted metal. He watched the gauge until the indicator dropped to a safe level, then shut it off, cutting the horrible screeching short and leaving in its wake a dead silence, eerie and unnerving. His eye caught Roberta's, and he realized they were both thinking the same thing.

"It *is* quiet," he said. "*Too* quiet. You wait here."

"Where are you going?" she demanded.

"See if I can take out that one guard. At least that'll give us a little room to maneuver." He stuffed his Luger into his belt and zipped his coat.

"Be careful," she said. It was an order, not a plea.

FIFTEEN

He eased out into the exposed area at the rear of the cabin, anxiously listening for the crackle of machine gun fire, but there was nothing except the hum of the wind across the opening. He glanced questioningly back at Roberta, then scampered down the narrow metal ladder and ran for the far end of the train, keeping to the shadows. The moon was at its zenith and with the help of the snow was lighting the landscape with a pale, opalescent daylight, which fortunately also created deep shadows.

He reached the last car, mounted another narrow ladder, and climbed to the roof. From here he leaped onto a rock shelf. The snow had been melting here all day and had refrozen, covering the rocks with a glasslike smoothness. He balanced carefully, trying to keep his weight directly over his feet, then rose up and latched on to an evergreen branch on the slope above. He took a step, balanced for a split second while he grabbed the next branch, then stepped again. In this way he was able to move mincingly, like a man on a tightrope, except that with only one good arm there was a gap when he moved from one branch to the next that left him vulnerable to falling. Several times he did almost fall, each time waving his hand frantically back and forth to keep himself upright until by some miracle it landed on another spiny twig and he was able to continue.

This little drama was being played out within easy range of

Kobelev's people, and Carter kept expecting the report of a rifle to come thundering over the snow along with the bullet that would crease his skull and send him toppling twenty feet to the tracks below or split his spine or whatever. But it didn't come, and he began to wonder if Kobelev had gone.

The rock shelf ended in a steep snowfield, prismatic in the moonlight, at the end of which protruded a finger of rock. This was where Carter expected to find him, and indeed *something* was leaning against the base of it, either a pack or a bundle—or a man. If it was a man, he was dead or asleep.

Carter pulled out his gun and made his way cautiously across the snow, but the surface of the field had frozen to a thin veneer of ice that cracked like glass underfoot. His footfalls sounded like depth charges in the stillness. *Christ! How could he not hear me?* Carter thought. But mercifully the wind was blowing up the mountain instead of down, carrying the crunch of Carter's footsteps out into the night.

As he drew closer he saw it definitely was a man hunched over with his arms folded in front of him.

He came still closer—to within pistol range—and thought surely now the man would see him. He stopped, ready to hit the snow if the man made a move. But nothing happened. It was as if the man were sleeping . . . or dead. He crept closer.

Finally, at a distance of about seventy-five feet, Carter realized the man was awake but slowly freezing to death. He was wearing only a light Windbreaker and no hat or gloves. His face was unearthly pale, his lips quivered, and his bald head was mottled with splotches of stark white. His eyes stared blankly forward, and although Carter had crossed his line of vision, the pupils remained unfocused.

With a sigh Carter let Wilhelmina fall limply to his side. It was no use killing a man who was already half dead. He would take him back to the train, have Roberta tie him up, and stick him in one of the back cars.

The man's eyes suddenly lit with the last remaining spark of realization of what was going on. He swung the big automatic rifle around, commencing fire at the beginning of his arc.

A spray of bullets went wide to Carter's left, spitting up tiny glistening geysers in the snow. Carter responded with a shot from the hip, cleaving the man's forehead dead center so forcefully and fast that it snapped back and his rifle discharged three shells harmlessly into the air. Then the man's big hulk slumped face-first into the snow, leaving little question as to the state of his health.

"Damn!" cursed Carter under his breath. He hadn't wanted to kill him. He lifted the corpse with the toe of his shoe. Snow was melting in rivulets on the still-warm face, and the eyes were open. It couldn't be helped. He picked up the rifle and slung it over his shoulder, then he stuffed Wilhelmina into his parka pocket and headed back toward the train.

Roberta was watching for him as he came up the tracks. "Nick!" she whispered hoarsely. "I heard gunshots."

"I wasn't on the receiving end," he said.

"Is he dead?"

"Very." He quickly climbed the ladder into the engine compartment. "Not that he stood much of a chance," he went on bitterly. "He was practically frozen stiff when I got there. Someday I'd like to find out what Kobelev does to these people to warrant such loyalty."

"Where do we go from here?" asked Roberta.

"We haven't heard anything from the other side for quite a while, have we?" said Carter, walking to the other side of the engine.

Roberta shook her head.

"Kobelev!" Carter yelled. The words echoed down the mountain.

There was no answer.

"Come on," said Carter, motioning to Roberta.

Carter took the frontal assault, climbing down out of the engine directly in line with Kobelev's position. Roberta went the other way, around the big boiler tank and over the tracks to try to outflank him. But again their precautions proved unnecessary. When they rounded the boulders, they found nothing but a wide area of churned-up snow and, in the middle, a slender girl with black hair wearing a man's too-large overcoat, lying on her side, trussed up like a roped calf. She was squirming and making muffled noises behind the cloth in her mouth, her relieved eyes telling them how glad she was to see them.

"Nick!" she shouted when they untied her. For a moment they sat in the snow holding each other without moving. Roberta crouched on her haunches.

"Why did they leave you behind?" Carter asked.

"Kobelev had Tatiana, so he fled on foot. He said if you had me maybe you would let him go."

"He must be dreaming! My orders are to kill him. I'll do it. He must know that. Which way did he go?"

She pointed up the track.

Carter followed her finger and shook his head, wondering what on earth Kobelev wanted in that direction. "How long ago?" he asked.

"Two hours. I don't know. Maybe a little longer."

Roberta broke in sympathetically. "You must be frozen clear through."

Carter and Roberta each gave her an arm and helped her up the ladder and into the engine room. While Cynthia warmed herself and got Roberta to tell her all that had happened while she'd been unconscious, Carter rummaged through the train, looking for anything he might be able to use in his pursuit of Kobelev. Within ten minutes he was back, his arms full.

"A gold mine," he muttered as he dropped it all with a clatter on the engine room floor. "Apparently, avalanches are fairly common along this section of track, and the train carries ample equipment in case the crew has to hike out of here."

On the floor were several pairs of snowshoes, three pick-axes, tents, an emergency stove, a bundle of flares, more coats and mittens, and two heavy-duty flashlights.

"There was even a shortwave radio," he said.

"Working?" asked Roberta hopefully.

Carter shook his head. "Sabotaged. Probably the first thing Kobelev did when he got on board. Oh—I found one other thing." He produced a large folded piece of paper from his back pocket. "A map," he said, spreading it on the floor.

"According to this, there's a town about twelve miles down the line. Doesn't look very big, though."

"It's got a phone no doubt, or a radio," said Roberta.

"You think that's where he's headed?"

Roberta nodded. "If I were him, I'd want to get out of here the quickest way I could."

"He said something about a town," put in Cynthia. "Alba . . . something."

"Alba Iulia," finished Carter. "That's it, then. I'd better get going. He's got a two-hour head start."

"Nick," Cynthia said, "take me with you."

Carter shook his head. "This is going to be very unpleasant work. And if you miss a cue, you'll get more than just a groan from the audience."

"I'm an experienced mountain climber, Nick. I spent most of my teen-age years in Colorado scaling rocks like Diamond Head and the north face of Long's Peak. I know what I'm doing."

"We're going to kill a man. Think you have the stomach for it?"

"That man, yes," she said resolutely.

"Well—" said Carter, starting to give in, but Roberta interrupted.

"May I speak with you alone?" she asked.

They descended the narrow steps out into the snow. When they were well out of Cynthia's earshot, Roberta confronted him. "You're thinking of taking her, aren't you?"

"I'd be a fool to go out there with only one good arm. I may need her."

"But she's an actress. She doesn't know the first thing about intelligence work."

"I'm certainly not going to leave the two of you here by yourselves. Kobelev may double back and make a try for the train. Now that I've got her back, I'm not going to leave her unprotected."

"But it's all right to leave me. Is that it?"

"You were trained for this sort of thing, Commander. She's an actress, remember?"

"And a damn good one."

"What's that supposed to mean?" asked Carter.

"I'm beginning to like you, Carter. I don't want to lose you."

Carter stepped closer, bent down, and their lips met. She tasted good. Cold, yet warm, almost burning in the center. For a moment Carter didn't want to let her go. When he finally stepped back, his heart was pounding. "Let's go back," he said, the words thick in his throat. "There are some things I want to check out with you before we go."

For the next half hour Carter conducted a crash course in train engineering, based on what little knowledge he had. He told her to keep the boiler pressure at the maximum in case she had to leave suddenly, and he showed her how to blow off steam to keep it from building too high. Then he pointed out the forward and reverse gears, and explained that in order to get through the avalanche she would have to back up to give herself some running room. With the melting during the day and the digging that was done, it would probably be possible to bust out, but only in an emergency.

He left her the machine gun and an extra clip of ammunition, then he and Cynthia dressed and went outside. They threw the snowshoes down beside the track and strapped them on. Roberta watched from the cab, looking like some sort of Tibetan guerrilla with her machine gun strapped over her filthy, snow-and-coal-encrusted parka and her smudged face. She waved when they left, and Carter continued to glance back over his shoulder to check on her until the train was out of sight.

Kobelev and his entourage had left a wide trail in the snow, and with the snowshoes and brilliant moonlight, Carter had high hopes of catching them. Cynthia turned out to be every inch the mountain woman she'd claimed to be. She plodded along beside him, matching him step for step, showing remarkable endurance for a creature of such slight build. And all this after her ordeal in the snow.

They found the first corpse about two hours later. They probably would have mistaken it for an exposed chunk of rock or a shrub if the evidence of the murder weren't so plainly visible in the snow.

The tracks indicated the group of them had been walking—Carter figured Kobelev, Tatiana, the two guards, the fireman, and the engineer—spread out, only loosely held together, and judging from the grooves extending from the toes of some prints, some staggering from exhaustion. They must have stopped to rest. Snow had been knocked off stones, and there were body prints on the ground. Carter was able to pick out Kobelev's footprints and Tatiana's, the smaller accompanying the larger wherever they went. They discussed something, briefly, for the prints were relatively few. Then one veered off from the others, long paces heading for a face of sheer rock, running with no place to run.

It was in following this set of footprints that they found him, face down in the snow with two bullets in his back, blood soaking his thick engineer's jacket, his hands outstretched, still wearing the long, cuffed gloves of his trade.

Cynthia was the first to reach him. "Nick! Look here!" she shouted, hopping over to it on her huge, tennis-racket shoes.

When Carter got there, he turned the body over. Blood had run from the nose and mouth and turned black against the abnormal whiteness of the face.

"God! Why did they shoot *him?*" she demanded, starting to whimper.

"Excess baggage maybe. I don't know."

Carter stared down at the body, trying to figure just why they *had* killed him. There was no evidence that one was falling behind the others. If anything, it was rather remarkable how well they'd hung together over such a long distance and such rough terrain. So why shoot him?

Carter told Cynthia to pull herself together. There was nothing they could do for this man now, and besides, she'd see plenty of this kind of thing soon, and she was going to have to be ready for it. She dried her eyes on her mittens, sniffed, and in a few minutes they were striding along much as before.

The silver disk of moon hung overhead, never moving or changing, and in time the path they were following and the hushed hills on either side seemed to become a place unto itself, without beginning or end, and even the memory of the engineer's death-mask face faded behind them. Then, half an hour after they'd found the first body, they came upon the second, sprawled in the middle of the trail, a bullet hole in his forehead.

"The fireman," Carter said to Cynthia who had turned away. "Must have been a small bore. I'd say he's been out here about an hour, maybe less. It's hard to tell in this cold."

"Nick," she said weakly, "I don't know if I can go on."

"Don't flake out on me now, sugar. Come on, they've run out of people to kill." He grabbed her by the hand, and soon they were tramping through the snow at twice the rate they had before.

It was a remarkable feat for the two of them: the man who had had little or no sleep the previous night and who had sustained serious injuries only recently; and the woman who herself had been through an extended ordeal. Yet they ran like two people possessed, as though they were being chased rather than chasing, as though the wooded hills themselves had suddenly become haunted. Carter, for one, sensed he was running *from* rather than *to,* and that his pursuer was as intangible as an idea that nagged at the back of his mind. Two murders for no clear motive suggested something wrong, terribly wrong, but he did not want to stop to consider what that something might be. Better to run and keep on running until at last, after thirty minutes and covering almost two miles, most of it uphill, he fell into the snow exhausted, panting like a winded dog.

Cynthia stood over him, blowing out huge clouds of vapor into the night air. "You all right?" she breathed.

"We're almost to the top. I've got a feeling we'll be able to see them from there."

Cynthia looked up. "Stay and rest. I'll go up for a look." She turned and plodded up the hill. He had just unstrapped his snowshoes when she shouted something and frantically gestured for him. He grabbed the snowshoes and scrambled up to her.

When he reached the top, he saw what she was screaming about. A hundred yards down the trail another body sat in the snow leaning against a rock. In the shadow it might have been mistaken for just another part of the rock except for the reflection of moonlight off the pure whiteness of its shaved head.

"Oh, my God," he muttered as he limped closer, for he sensed the nagging realization that what he'd just spent the last half hour eluding was about to thrust itself upon him, the implications of which were going to be very painful when sorted out.

"Nick! Nick!" Cynthia shouted. She covered her face with her mittens.

He took her in his arms and held her close for several moments. "It's all right, Cynthia," he said soothingly.

She stopped calling his name but continued to cry quietly into her mittens.

There was something definitely very wrong here. He could feel it thick in the chill air. He began to pace furiously, finally pulling up short, and it was a measure of his agitation that it had taken him this long to notice the obvious. "He committed suicide!"

It was true. The corpse still held the means of its destruction in its hand, a .22-caliber handgun that had put a small hole in the right temple and a slightly larger hole in the left side near the crown, creating two continents of blood on a globe of otherwise perfectly blank sea.

"What does it mean?" Cynthia asked weakly.

"I'm not sure," said Carter, slumping onto the rock opposite the corpse. "Hold it!" he shouted suddenly. He jumped up and began running up and down in the snow. "Where are they? I don't see them."

"What? What are you looking for?"

"The footprints! Tatiana's and Kobelev's! I don't see them! I haven't seen them since . . . since that first body. We veered off the trail there, and when we came back, they were gone. A diversion! Leading us on from corpse to corpse while he makes his escape. The train!"

He came wearily back to the rock and sat down. Cynthia plopped down into the snow. She'd stopped crying. She merely looked at him now with a strange steadfastness.

Moments passed while Carter stared into the snow at his feet and sighed. But Cynthia never moved. She leveled her gaze on his face with an absorbing interest.

Finally she began to get on his nerves. "What are you staring at?" he asked shortly. "My defeat? Is that what fascinates you so much? Did you think I was above that sort of thing? Well, I'm not. I can't beat him! I've tried and I can't do it."

"I've waited a long time to hear you say that," said Cynthia, only it wasn't Cynthia's voice. It was a good deal deeper, throatier, with a hard edge to it that told the listener its owner could just as easily kill a man as love him.

"Tatiana!" he said, scarcely daring to breathe the word.

"Correct." She smiled a little, producing a pearl-handled revolver from her mitten. The handle glinted in the moonlight.

SIXTEEN

"You and your father must have planned this little surprise right from the beginning," said Carter with a forced laugh. A chill sweat glistened on his forehead in spite of the cold. He had to think, to assess the situation. Kobelev had an hour's head start on a two-hour trip back to the train. Carter would have to make an all-out push to beat him there, but first he was going to have to get the gun away from Tatiana.

"Actually, it was my idea," she said. "Papa wanted to take the train back by force, but when I saw that that girl looked just like me, had my exact face, same eyes, teeth, hair—everything the same—I persuaded him to help me create this little ruse to get you out here alone."

"Vengeance means a great deal to you, doesn't it?"

"I've wanted you dead for a long time, Carter. Ever since—"

"Ever since that night we slept together in your father's *dacha?*" Carter said, finishing her thought. "Don't give yourself away any too easily, do you, Tatiana? See a man you like, feel some attraction for, and you're threatened down to the soles of your shoes, isn't that so?"

"I never really liked you, Carter. I hated you on sight."

"Really? As I remember, I didn't come to you that night, you came to me. And don't try to tell me your father put you up to it, because you almost bollixed his plans by doing it. No, you wanted me all right, and you still want me, and because you think you can never have me, you want to kill me. Isn't that true?"

"No," she said firmly. "I hate you."

"A dying man has a right to find out the truth before he meets his end, doesn't he? If I'm to be killed by an insanely jealous woman, I have a right to know it, haven't I?"

"I am not jealous!" she shouted, rising to her feet. "You . . . you are trying to provoke me, to get me to make a mistake. You see? I know all your tricks."

"I'm not tricking you," Carter said calmly. "If there's no truth to what I'm saying, why are you so angry?"

"I am *not* angry!" she snapped.

"Let's face it, Tatiana, you've been in love with me right from the start. You haven't been able to think of anything else. And you hate me because you think I could never return those feelings. You think I laugh at you behind your back."

She stopped pacing and scrutinized him closely. "You do laugh at me. I know it. But very soon you will not laugh anymore."

"You are wrong, Tatiana. I don't laugh. Not at all. I rather enjoyed that night we spent together. I've thought about it often."

"You are lying!" she shouted.

"What reason would I have to lie now? I'm a dead man, remember? You misjudge yourself. You are far more beautiful than you imagine. Although I can understand how you might not know it. With a father as powerful as yours, how could you be sure any man would tell you the truth?"

This last sentence had an almost physical effect. Her head rose slightly, and her expression sobered. "At least there are some things you understand," she said.

Carter sensed she'd taken the bait. The trick now was to keep the line taut and let her reel herself in. "Where is Cynthia now?" he asked, changing the subject. "Still with your father?"

"Yes, I think she amuses him. She looks exactly like me, you know." There was a pause, then she asked: "Did you ever make love to her, Carter?"

"Yes, several times."

"And did you notice she looked like me?"

"The thought crossed my mind."

"And did it stimulate you?"

"You mean, did I find it erotic that she reminded me of you? I don't think you have any right to ask that."

"No right? I have the gun, you forget. I have all the right in the world. Now answer the question."

"All right," said Carter after a short pause, "it *was* stimulating. I remembered the night we were together, the things you liked to do, the way you are . . ." He gestured vaguely, implying this was too vast to describe.

"And what way is that?"

"Oh," he said, looking off down the mountain as though written there somewhere were a way to describe her wondrousness but noticing, as he did so, that she'd come several steps closer, "one has the feeling that there is much untapped in you, Tatiana. A volcano just below the surface. One wonders what might happen if that fire were ever unleashed."

"And did it drive you to new heights of passion?" she asked, staring down at him, breathing heavily.

"Yes." He said the word softly as though she had torn it from his heart, so softly, in fact, she couldn't hear it.

"What?" she asked, leaning closer.

He saw his chance and he took it. Grabbing his snowshoe by its edge, he swung hard, aiming for her head. She pulled back, but he made contact with the pistol and knocked it aside. It went off, burying a bullet in the trunk of a nearby tree.

She fell back and he fell on top of her, desperately trying to grab the gun before she could point it at him again. Unfortunately, she was right-handed, and his right was the only hand Carter had. He was forced to reach across her, which left her left hand open to scratch and pull and hit.

He managed to finally get a hold of her wrist, but she was a good deal stronger than he supposed. Although he could prevent her from twisting it toward him, he couldn't get her to drop it, no matter how much pressure he applied. She suddenly wrenched her leg away and brought it back sharply.

A flood of nauseating pain welled up from his bowels, the world spun, and his stomach turned inside out. The strength drained from his arms, and he felt the gun slip from his grasp.

In desperation he realized he had only one option. He settled on top of her, praying she was more interested in killing him with the gun than trying to kick his balls off again.

She made muffled shouts against his parka. He still fumbled for the gun even though he'd lost track of it. Then he found it, pressed against his chest, just as it discharged with a muted *pop* between them.

He lay there wondering if he were hit and if so, how bad. How would he know with waves of agony coursing up his spine and out to every finger and toe? Then he realized Tatiana wasn't moving, hadn't moved, and wasn't breathing either.

He rolled off her. The pearl-handled gun lay across her chest, and a growing stain of blood seeped from her coat. He guessed the bullet had gone straight into her heart, she'd died so fast.

He pulled himself unsteadily to his feet, leaned back on the stone where he'd been sitting, and put his head between his knees to try to keep from being sick.

Kobelev was an hour from the train. He had no snowshoes and was probably dragging Cynthia, who would be doing her best to slow him down. Still, it would be impossible for Carter to overtake him. Only a miracle would get him back there in time.

A spasm twisted in his gut, and his worries about Kobelev, the tension he'd felt in front of Tatiana's gunsight, and the rolls he'd eaten with Roberta back at the train all ended up in a steaming puddle in front of him. When it passed, he wiped his mouth and washed his face with snow and told himself he felt better, even if he wasn't sure it was true.

He went over and took the pistol from Tatiana's hand and stuffed it in his coat pocket. Then he stood for a moment, staring down at the monk who had given his life to bring this little rendezvous about. What had Kobelev promised him that was worth killing himself for? Carter wondered.

He passed it off with a shrug, located his wayward snowshoe, and stooped down to strap it on. Then he looked down the long line of snowshoe prints that started at the top of the hill and extended better than ten miles back to the railroad and the Orient Express. There was no way he'd be able to trudge all that distance in less than an hour.

Then he wondered what would have happened if Tatiana had killed him as planned? She certainly wasn't going to walk all the way back to meet her father. And he wasn't going to pick her up with the train. There was no sign of a railroad track anywhere.

On a hunch he circled the area around the big rock that now served as a headstone. On the western side of the trail about a hundred feet out he came across a line of partially brushed-out footprints. He followed them to a pair of cross-country skis behind a tree. The monk had apparently stashed them here for Tatiana before blowing his brains out.

They were a woman's size. Consequently, the boots accompanying them were hopelessly small. But the bindings could be adjusted around his own snow boots and in a few minutes, he was poling his way one-handed to the top of the hill.

He stood at the crest for a moment, surveying the expanse of snow that stretched out before him, then with a thrust, he pushed himself out onto the mountain, kicking at first to gain speed, then curling into the aerodynamically efficient "egg" position for minimum wind resistance. It was a good thing, he thought, one never forgot how to ski.

For Lieutenant Commander j.g. Roberta Stewart, waiting had always been an anathema. As a child of five she remembered the long hours of delay while bureaucratic wranglings kept her father in the Hungarian State Prison long after his sentence as an insurgent during the revolution of 1956 had been put down. She remembered the long plane ride and the hours of questioning by immigration authorities before they finally let her father and herself out of the terminal at Idlewild. And later on, she'd waited three days longer than any OCS candidate to get her commission—only to discover to her joy and trepidation that she'd been assigned back to the country of her birth. There had been many anxious moments of waiting since then, waiting for messages to be picked up in letter drops around the American consulate, waiting in alleys to talk to contacts, the disgruntled dock worker, the Soviet official cheating on his wife who thought she would make a fetching sexual trophy (and who never succeeded but, in trying, always spilled his guts of everything he knew). Waiting had become her life, and yet of all the nervous hours she had spent in anticipation of things both good and bad, none of them held a candle to the hours she spent waiting for Nick Carter to return to the Orient Express.

Outside the train the wind whistled up from the valley below with a low, mournful moan that set her teeth on edge. The old wooden cars creaked and settled on the track, and every stray noise made her jump and clutch her machine gun.

She sat on the floor of the engine room, her back to the fire doors, the machine gun resting across her knees. From time to time she would crawl the few feet to the coal supply, retrieve an armful, and toss them into the furnace. Then she would slam the doors and resume the same tense, watchful pose as before.

The boiler became more than just a source of warmth. It was her ticket out of here, she told herself, and if she took care of it, it would take care of her. She believed this, and the hot metal became a benign, almost friendly, sensation at her back, like the warm lap of a parent when all the world around has turned hostile and cold.

Her thoughts centered mostly on Nick, on how he was doing, if he would ever come back to her, and what she would do if he didn't. She told herself she definitely didn't love him, although even before the words had fully formed in her mind, she knew it was a lie. And yet she knew, too, that love between them was impossible. They were two professionals, each with his job to do. They would love briefly, and they would say good-bye, and their love would be sweeter and more poignant because of it. These were her thoughts, but in the cold darkness of the engine cabin, her heart spun out fantasies of the two of them running, laughing into a pounding tropical surf as though they hadn't a care in the world.

Minutes crept by. Time seemed to pass like sand in an hourglass, one infinitesimal grain at a time. Occasionally she would think she couldn't stand it any longer, and she would pace the cabin and strain to see if there weren't two figures trudging toward her at the head of a long column of footprints that would signal her vigil had finally come to an end. Once, by some convoluted reasoning, she even fired a machine gun burst into the air, thinking it might help lead them home. It was only frustration expressing itself, and when she thought of the possibility of the gunshots starting another avalanche, she was horrified. She took up her position in front of the furnace again and vowed not to leave it until Nick himself pried her away.

The hours marched by and sleep tempted her, although the ache in her stomach kept it from being much of a threat. She hadn't eaten since Nick had found the lunch box with the rolls, and although since then she'd gone back and licked the wrappers, it had far from satisfied her, and her stomach had groaned for more. But when nothing was forthcoming, it eventually grew quiet until it lay dormant between her ribs and she forgot about it. Then sleep tugged on her more and more insistently, so that when she heard the first of the cries, she wasn't sure whether it was real or she'd been asleep and dreamed it.

By the second cry, there was no possibility of mistake. Someone was out there in the dark. A woman in trouble. She first thought it was Cynthia returning without Nick, and a stab of cold went through her. But then she realized whoever it was didn't know her name, and she felt confused and afraid.

She pressed herself against the wall by the brakeman's window and quickly glanced outside. In the snow one hundred feet away stood a woman about the same height and general coloring as Cynthia, only dressed in furs. "Help!" she yelled for what was now the third time.

"Who is it?" Roberta shouted, being careful to keep her

head well back out of any line of fire.

"Cynthia Barnes. A friend of Nick Carter's. You speak English?"

"Of course I speak English. But you're lying. You're not Cynthia Barnes. Nick left here with Cynthia Barnes about three hours ago. You must be. . ."

"No! Nick was fooled! *I'm* Cynthia Barnes. When he came to get me to take this assignment, I was working on a production of *A Streetcar Named Desire*. Shall I do a few lines to prove it to you?"

At this moment, against all her training, Lieutenant Commander j.g. Roberta Stewart committed a momentary lapse of security. In the parlance, she "dropped her guard." The thought of Nick out somewhere on the mountain at the mercy of Tatiana Kobelev (for who else could it have been masquerading as Cynthia?) so startled her, she stepped into full view in the window. A shot sounded, like a brief thunderclap, somewhere below and to her right. There was a sharp sensation on her head, as though she'd stepped into a whirling propeller blade, and she flew backward.

She lay on the floor, conscious but unable to move, listening as powerful footsteps mounted the metal ladder into the compartment.

"My God, she's still alive!" cried Cynthia, her voice strident. She was scared out of her wits.

"It's of no matter," said another voice, masculine this time, and while there was no accent, Roberta noticed schoolbook English.

Strong hands took hold of her arms at the elbows and dragged her to the opening. Then she plummeted to the snow.

"You can't just leave her like that!" said Cynthia, tears filling her eyes.

There was a short derisive laugh from the man. "You're quite right. It's most uncivilized of me. But there simply isn't time to call an ambulance. We must be going."

"Aren't you going to wait for your daughter?"

More laughter amid the cranking of valves being opened and the hiss of steam. "You understand nothing of what I've been telling you. I've trained Tatiana to master any situation.

Did she not escape the United States under the heaviest security possible? Did she not find me on the Orient Express in the middle of western Hungary? It is a game we play, she and I. It keeps us strong."

The engine whistle sounded, signifying the boiler was ready. The enormous pushrods extended and fell to, and the ground beneath Roberta shook as the huge train began to move down the track.

SEVENTEEN

Carter found her almost by accident, lying face down in the snow, thrown there so carelessly, her machine gun was still strapped to her back, standing on end with its muzzle in the air. It was the machine gun that led him to her. He'd seen it as he approached, thinking it was another of the shovels Kobelev and crew had been using to clear the track. Then he'd noticed the lump beneath it was the same color as Roberta's parka.

It was hard to say how long she'd been there. Thirty minutes, maybe more. Her lips were blue and her cheeks had a bloodless, ivory pallor that frightened him at first. But as he rubbed her hands and slapped her, buds of color began to appear under the skin. Soon she felt warm, and in a few minutes she opened her eyes.

"Oh," she moaned as she reached for the streak of blood that ran along the side of her head.

"Don't touch it," he said, gently pulling her hand back. "It's just a scratch. You were very lucky."

"Nick!" she cried, suddenly remembering what had happened. "You're alive! I thought Tatiana—"

"Was going to kill me? She tried, but she got distracted."

"Did you . . . ?"

Carter nodded. "I did. The others are dead, too. Including the engineer and the brakeman."

"Kobelev was here. He had Cynthia with him. They took the train."

"I know. Don't upset yourself. They haven't got much of a lead."

"But how are we . . . ?"

"Trust me."

He helped her to stand, then picked her up in a fireman's carry over his shoulder.

"Nick!" she exclaimed. "Are you strong enough for this?"

"Don't worry about me," he said with a grunt. "But do me a favor. Don't gain any weight en route."

He carried her, staggering only slightly, until she said she felt up to walking, in fact walking would probably be less strenuous than bouncing on his shoulder like a sack of flour. By this time they were half a mile around the curve in the track. He put her down, and when she turned around her eyes lit up with surprise.

"A helicopter!" she gasped. "Where did it come from?"

"I sort of boosted it from the Hungarian People's Army. They were going to deport me in it. Can you fly?"

"You bet. Part of my naval training."

"Good," Carter said. They climbed up into the cockpit and strapped in. He watched her as she studied the instruments and controls. "Are you going to be able to handle this?"

She looked at him and nodded, then turned back, started the machine, and they lifted off. They found the train within a few minutes, steaming along on a relatively flat, open section of track.

"This is the place to intercept him," Nick said. "The wind here isn't so irregular that you'll have trouble holding us steady. Just match his speed somewhere over the middle of the train. With the noise of that steam engine, he probably won't even know we're here."

A bullet smacked against the windshield as he spoke, creating a spider web of cracks. "Guess I was wrong," Carter shouted. "Don't worry about it. Just hold it steady. It's me he wants, anyway."

Carter unstrapped himself and went below. A thick rope ladder hung in a coil from the bulkhead. He brought it down, moored it to the floor of the chopper, then slid open the big side door and threw it out. It landed on the train below, twisting back and forth in the chopper's wash.

He checked the Luger, took off the safety, and stuffed it in his pants. Then he pulled it out again quickly. He wanted to make sure it drew without a hitch. He'd been hampered before by as minuscule a thing as a loose thread, and he wanted to make damn sure it didn't happen again.

He climbed out on the ladder and hesitated for a split second, looking down at the swaying car. This was the dangerous part. From here until he lit on the car's roof, he was a sitting duck. There was no place to hide, and with only one usable arm he couldn't return fire.

Taking a deep breath, he started down as fast as he could.

Kobelev fired a steady barrage into the air, but the ladder whipped back and forth, making Carter a poor target. He was halfway down before Kobelev was able to hit anything, and then it was only sheer luck that a bullet tore through the side of the ladder, shredding most of its strands. It held for a second, then collapsed, leaving Carter dangling by one hand, his feet swinging wildly looking for rungs that were no longer there.

Kobelev increased the density of his fire pattern. He had an automatic and was splayed out on the top of the coal heap behind the engine.

A bullet split the sleeve of Carter's parka. Then Kobelev stopped and took careful aim. In spite of the noise and the constant freezing wind, Carter felt sweat under his arms as the gunsight zeroed in on him. This time Kobelev wouldn't miss. Carter glanced down. Fifteen feet to the train. He'd never make the jump without falling off.

Then suddenly the copter dipped forward. His first impression was that Roberta had made some sort of error, as he came hurtling toward the car roof. He landed hard but managed to stay aboard by clinging to the rope.

Then he realized Roberta's plan had been much more daring. Judging the distance between the copter's rotor and Kobelev, she had tried to dip the rotor enough to foul his shot. It was a brave move, but foolish. At that angle the rotor's blades were no longer able to work enough air to keep her aloft. The chopper came down on its nose with a crunch. The rotor blades whacked against the coal tender and sheered. It bounced its wheels on the car's top just over Carter's head, then slipped off the train altogether. It landed on its top and rolled alongside the track for several hundred feet, finally ending on its side with its tail pointed crazily toward the sun. Carter watched for several anxious seconds, but it lay there inert, no explosion, no flames.

Kobelev had started shooting again, this time with a vengeance; bullets filled the air over Carter's head. Carter rolled over, brought out the Luger, but remembering he had only a few cartridges left, he held his fire.

In a few seconds the stream of gunfire abruptly stopped. Carter heard the telltale clicking of a spent magazine. This was it. The moment he'd been waiting for. He pulled himself to his feet, swaying to keep his balance on the speeding train, and started forward.

Kobelev was thirty feet in front of him, his gun leveled as though it still held bullets. Behind him, Cynthia lay curled on the floor of the engine cabin, staring dumbly at the passing countryside, the events of the last few hours having reduced her to catatonia.

"Give it up, Kobelev!" Carter yelled.

"Where's my daughter?" Kobelev yelled back. "What have you done with Tatiana?"

"She tried to kill me."

"So you killed her instead. You're going to die for that, Carter." Kobelev pulled the trigger. The gun discharged, the bullet striking the Luger along the barrel and knocking it out of Carter's hand. It flew back off the train and Carter stared after it dumbfounded.

"You thought my gun was empty? Did you honestly think I'd be so foolish as to leave myself without a weapon?"

Kobelev took careful aim, this time at Carter's midsection. There was no time to jump aside, no time to do anything. He pulled the trigger. The gun failed to fire. He pulled again and again. It clicked harmlessly.

"I'd say you jammed it," said Carter.

Angrily Kobelev threw the weapon. "I'll tear you to pieces with my bare hands," Kobelev shouted, scrambling up the coal pile and jumping the short distance to the first car.

They now stood face to face, eye to eye, legs slightly bent and separated to keep themselves from falling.

"You're done," shouted Carter.

They took a few steps closer, like wary heavyweights feeling each other out, both wanting to inflict damage but neither wanting to sustain any.

Meanwhile, the train sped on. They were coming to a bridge. The timberwork overhead looked as though it would pass within a few feet of the car roofs, much less than the six or seven feet necessary to clear a standing man. Off to the left was the froth of a tumbling stream, not yet frozen in mid-October.

Carter watched the bridge drawing closer. Then he looked at Kobelev's face. Eyes narrowed, jaw set in grim determination to avenge his daughter's death.

Kobelev closed in, his hands circling in front of him like claws with which to grab Carter and throw him from the train. Behind him the bridge timbers rushed at them. At the very last moment, Carter dived onto the car top.

"You can't fool me, Carter . . ." Kobelev's words were cut off by the sickening thud of dull wood against bone. He was slammed facedown on the car, the back of his head little more than a raw flap of skin. Carter, who lay only a few feet away, reached out to hold the body, but before he could get a grip, the vibration of the train moved it to the edge, and it slipped out of his grasp. Kobelev hit the ties below and rolled into the icy froth of the river.

Then the river had its way, tumbling and smashing the body against rocks, burying it in torrents of foam. The train took a sharp curve around a bend of mountain and the river disappeared. The cars pitched far to the outside, and Carter realized the train was traveling too fast for the grade. The angle of the cars was so great that he had to hang on to the roof beam by his fingertips.

When it finally straightened out, he pulled himself back up and scrambled down the car to the engine. Cynthia was still sitting on the floor, unmoved and unmoving, oblivious to what was happening around her. When he approached she looked up, flinching as though she expected to be hit.

"Easy, girl," he said softly. He put a hand on her shoulder, and her face suddenly lit up with recognition.

"Nick!" She reached out for him, but he pulled away.

"I've got to slow us down first." He went to the control panel and pulled out the piece of wood Kobelev had used to jam the throttle. The engine slowed immediately, but the train's momentum and the grade were still pulling it along too fast.

He applied the brake. A horrible screeching filled the air, and sparks rose from the wheels as they fought the track. But she slowed, gradually but unmistakably. It took him all of fifteen minutes to get her stopped completely. By this time Cynthia was at his side, her face buried in the collar of his parka, weeping uncontrollably.

Difficult as it was for her to speak, she managed to squeeze out a few words: "There's a girl back on the track. Kobelev shot her, but she didn't die. She's lying there all alone."

"I know. We're going back to get her now." He put the engine in reverse and began to slowly push the fifteen empty cars back up the hill.

It was rough going until they reached the bridge, then the road bed flattened and they began to pick up speed. In a few minutes they were back on the straightaway, and the overturned helicopter became visible on the snowfield. As they approached, a figure emerged, waving.

"Hurry up, Stewart," Carter shouted when he finally got it stopped. "You're holding up the train."

Roberta quickly climbed the narrow ladder to the engine.

"Roberta Stewart, this is Cynthia Barnes, actress extraordinaire, and lately, girl hostage."

"Nice to meet the real you," said Roberta.

"Nice to see you're alive and well," Cynthia said, smiling.

"Now," said Carter, putting his right arm around Roberta and kissing Cynthia on the cheek. "Do you suppose the two of you could go back into the dining car and rustle up something for us to eat while I get this train moving again?"

They nodded.

"Good. Next stop, Istanbul."

DON'T MISS THE NEXT NEW NICK CARTER SPY THRILLER

THE DECOY HIT

The only sound in the barn was that of the car's running motor. Nick sat with his back against the car, Stephanie's gun in his right hand. Suddenly, in this closed area, the gun became more of a weapon and less of a toy. He looked above at the hayloft, hoping that when he had seen the man at the barn door it hadn't been some kind of trick of the sun. If he was right, his rented car was now between himself and the killer.

Moving up on his haunches he eased down toward the front of the car so that he was up against a wheel. That prevented his being shot underneath the car. He held the gun ready, counted to three and then stood up and braced himself on the hood of the car with the gun held out in front of him.

One of the barn doors was hanging on one hinge, the top one, and was still swaying from the force of Nick's entry. Scanning the wall opposite him he saw that there wasn't anyplace to hide, yet the man who had been shooting at them was nowhere in sight.

Had he gotten out of the barn immediately after Nick's entry?

If he had gotten out he was either long gone, or he'd gone to the house, in which case he now had Stephanie. Nick was too much of a pro to let that thought send him rushing out from his cover. He was going to act on the assumption that the killer was there in the barn with him, until he proved otherwise.

Slowly, holding the gun out in front of him, he began to move out from behind the car, which was busily filling the air inside the barn with carbon monoxide. There were too many holes in the structure of the barn—not to mention the open door—for it to be deadly, but it was getting uncomfortable.

Nick made a slow circuit of the barn with his eyes, spotting no one. There were two alternatives. Either the killer was in the hayloft—or he was behind the door that was hanging on one hinge, waiting for his chance.

Nick didn't think he was in the hayloft. He was sure he'd seen the man at the door, and he hadn't had time to run up the ladder before Nick drove into the barn.

He was behind the door, then, waiting. If Nick approached the door to pull it shut, the killer could shoot him easily. Firing his own gun through the door was too chancy. He could use up his loads and still not hit the man. Besides that, the .25 might not have sufficient power to penetrate the door.

What he had to do was decoy the man into pushing the door shut himself.

The ladder to the hayloft was wood, and it appeared to be unstable. If a man tried to climb it, it would surely rattle, make a noise. Nick backed his way to it, keeping his front covered. Reaching behind him he stopped when he encountered the ladder with his left hand. Then, tightening his grip on the gun, he rattled the ladder, hoping that it would sound as if he were climbing it, which he'd normally have to do with his back to the barn door.

He also hoped there was no crack in the door that a man could see between.

As the ladder rattled, the door suddenly swung shut, propelled by the power of a kick. The killer, after standing with his back to the wall for so long, stepped forward and pointed his rifle at the ladder, where he expected to find Nick's back.

—From *The Decoy Hit*
A New Nick Carter Spy Thriller
From Charter in October